THE STORY BOX

Also by Monica Hughes

THE
STORY BOX

MONICA HUGHES

HarperCollins*PublishersLtd*

http://www.harpercanada.com

HarperCollins books may be purchased for educational,
business, or sales promotional use. For information please write:
Special Markets Department, HarperCollins Canada,
Suite 2900, 55 Avenue Road, Toronto,
Canada M5R 3L2.

First published in trade paper by HarperCollins in 1998
First mass market edition

Canadian Cataloguing in Publication Data

Hughes, Monica, 1925–
The story box

ISBN 0-00-648505-7

I. Title

PS8565.U34S76 1999   jC813'.54   C98-931384-0
PZ7.H83St 1999

---

01 02 03 04 OPM 6 5 4 3
Printed and bound in the United States

To the Storytellers who remember what is important
With love and respect

For Alyssa

Best wishes

Marcia Hughes

May 12, 2001

CHAPTER ONE

*She was with them only between the newing and the
olding of the moon, but was never forgotten,
though spoken of secretly and in whispers.*

It was on a Sunday night, when a great storm swept
in from the west, lashing the shore with angry waves
and rattling the shutters of the houses in Merton
Town. It was a storm with a chorus of many voices,
carrying on it the memories of snapped masts and
torn sails, sails whose sodden weight could pull the
small square-rigged fishing boats down into the
depths, where the bones of the sailors would lie
forever among the rotting hulls of other wrecks.

As the fifty or so houses that clustered around
Merton Harbour creaked and groaned in the gale,
men and women stirred, awoke, and remembered the
lost fishermen of their own families. The wives
counted husbands and sons safe in their beds and,

with thanks to the Almighty, recalled that the fleet was at anchor this night in the secure harbour. Then they shivered, pulled the covers over their heads to hide the screaming voices of the storm, and went back to sleep.

In the house of Fergus the shepherd and his wife Hedda, their son Colin woke with a start. He had heard the wind many times, but tonight it had a different voice, a high keening note that seemed very close—as if it were right inside the attic. Like a child crying in fear . . .

Etta!

He threw aside his warm quilt and jumped out of bed, his toes curling back from the cold floor. He padded across the attic and pushed aside the woollen curtain that separated his bedroom from that of his younger sister. He groped towards the bed. She was sitting bolt upright, her hands clutching her quilt, her mouth opened in yet another wail.

Quickly he smothered her cry with his hand, feeling her hot cheeks, wet with tears. "Ssh, Etta. It's only a storm."

She shook herself free of his hand. "No," she gasped, "not the storm. Horrible beasts with scales and long teeth. Coming to get me!"

Colin felt a cold fear in his stomach. This was not the first time Etta had woken up speaking of the unspeakable. "It's only the wind," he whispered assurance. "Nothing else. Just the wind."

She shook her head again, but snuggled up against his chest, clinging to his nightshirt with hot damp hands. Slowly her sobs diminished to hiccups. "It was a bad dream," she whispered. "A horrid bad dream."

Again he put his hand over her mouth. "Hush, Etta. There are no such things as dreams. Nor creatures with scales and teeth. You know that."

She pulled his hand away. "But I saw . . ."

He shivered. "Be quiet. You saw nothing. You will tell no one about this 'nothing'. Not Mother or Father or your friends. Promise?" He shook her shoulders gently, swallowing the panic that rose in his throat. The *danger* she was putting them in!

"But . . ."

"Promise, Etta."

She sniffed back tears. "If you promise to stay with me till I go to sleep," she whispered cunningly.

"I will." He made her lie down and tucked the quilt around her. "Now you will think good *true* thoughts," he told her sternly as he smoothed the tangle of hair from her face. "Think about the last picnic we had up at South Peak."

"I picked berries," she said sleepily. "More berries than anyone."

"So you did." He stroked her forehead. "And ate the most too."

She gave a faint chuckle. Her eyelids fluttered and closed. He kept his hand on her forehead, straining his ears through the racket of the storm, hoping that his parents had not heard Etta's crying. The attic was far enough away from their bed downstairs that it was unlikely that Hedda or Fergus would have heard anything above the voice of the storm. It was important that they didn't. Lucky for Etta that he'd woken before her cries had disturbed them.

When was the last time that one of the young people had been caught breaking the Law? At least ten years, he reckoned. He'd been a child himself, Colin remembered—younger than Etta was now. And the youth, from the village of Lynn-by-the-Lake, had been perhaps fourteen, a white-faced young man whose freckles showed startlingly against his pale cheeks. He had been locked up on a diet of bread and water until he had been purged of his wickedness and then judged by the Moot, so it had been rumoured. What was his name? What had become of him? *How strange that I've forgotten*, thought Colin.

Etta's even breathing told him that she was sound asleep. Before leaving, he went over to the window to fasten the shutter. It was its rattling, he felt sure, that had disturbed her. It was made of ancient wood—the hatch cover from some long-ago wreck thrown up on the shore of their island—and the iron nails fastening the latch had worked loose. Time it was replaced, Colin thought. He would take a trip to Half-Moon Cove tomorrow to see if the storm had thrown ashore any useful pieces of wood from which he might fashion a more secure shutter for his sister's window.

Back in the warmth of his own bed, he rubbed his icy feet, his thoughts turning once more to Etta. She was a worrisome child, given to forbidden flights of imagination; her "dreams" were the most worrisome of all, and he wondered how long he would be able to hide them from their parents—and from the Elders. He shivered at the thought of the Elders finding out. *Ariban is the most beautiful island in the ocean*, he told himself firmly, *and we are indeed fortunate to live here. But the Elders must be obeyed.*

Just before sliding into sleep, he remembered the name of the boy who had been punished: Alan. An unlucky name which had not been used since that time.

Colin woke early, with the plan to go to Half-Moon Cove still fresh in his mind. When he pushed back the shutter, the air rushed into the stuffy attic, filling it with the tangy scent of the sea. The storm had blown over, and the world outside his tiny window looked newly washed in the watery grey of dawn. His window faced north and, looking past the last few cottages on the outskirts of Merton, he could see the grazing grounds, shrouded in early morning mist, rolling away into the distance.

He pulled on woollen breeches and shirt, tucked his knife in its leather sheath into the top of one of the thick socks his mother had knitted for him, and put on a sheepskin jerkin fashioned with the wool on the inside. With his shoes in his hand he tiptoed downstairs.

His mother and father were still asleep in the curtained bed next to the fire. In the stone hearth the peat fire smouldered, and the pot of porridge that Hedda had set on the hob last night was still hot. He stirred down the skin on the top, spooned out a bowlful, and ate it while standing, warming his calves at

5

the remnant of the fire. When he was done he took a small loaf and a wedge of cheese from the larder, wrapped them in a clean cloth, and tied the bundle to his belt. He looked around. What else might he need?

Several coils of thin rope hung from hooks under the ceiling. He lifted down a piece long enough to bind together any cast-up wood he might be fortunate enough to find and slung it over his shoulder.

Then he lifted the latch and stepped quietly out into the spring morning.

The cobbled streets of Merton Town were shiny with dew, dangerously slippery under the soles of leather shoes. In his socked feet he walked north to the last row of houses, to where the road gave way to a grassy track, and here he stopped to slip on his shoes and tie the thongs securely.

Looking back over the town, Colin could see that every cottage door and shutter was still tightly closed against the night air. From each chimney came only the faint thread of blue-grey smoke, smelling sweetly of the damped-down peats that had smouldered through the night. With a triumphant bound of his heart he realized that he was indeed the first person awake in Merton Town. Unless someone from the village of Lynn-by-the-Lake had the same idea, he would be the first person to reach Half-Moon Cove and claim any bounty that might be salvaged from the storm.

Not just bounty for his family. At Midsummer, after his sixteenth birthday, he and Gwynne were to be married. It was a point of honour to bring as much as possible to furnish their future home. Why, he might find enough good wood to fashion a table! Gwynne was the granddaughter of Elder Fisher, and a person of some importance in Merton Town. It would be good to impress her. He felt a sense of great adventure waiting for him around the corner, a feeling that came on him every time he was up and about before everyone else.

Briskly he set out, climbing steadily up the gentle valley side, away from the town and the river flowing down to it from Lynn Lake. On his right, just a stone's throw away, was the moot ground, the Judgement Stone rising like a dark shadow on its southern slope. Now used only at Midsummer to set the price of wool and to settle the occasional disagreement over grazing rights, the moot ground was still regarded with awe. Children did not play down there, nor were the sheep allowed to graze on its lush grass.

Once he reached the pastureland above the valley of Merton, he stopped to look back again. From this flat tabletop, he could view the sea in every direction except to the southwest, where the swell of South Peak obscured it. The Isle of Ariban was like a grey-green platter floating on a grey sea, a sea that met the pale grey sky in a blurred line of mist.

As he stood, rejoicing in his island home—surely the best place in the whole world in which to live—he saw a blush of rose-pink run up the eastern sky, staining the sea beneath it. Soon the sun would be up and people stirring. No time to waste standing here. His way led along a track to the northwest, only a thin trail trampled through grass and heath, barely visible in the half light.

Few people came this way, because there was no safe harbour on the west coast. The cliffs were high and the shoreline jagged with rocks. In the spring, sea birds nested here in their thousands, and townsfolk unafraid of heights swung dizzily down to the nests to claim their eggs; in summertime, the women scoured the rocky shores to gather great baskets full of seaweed. For the rest of the year the path was unused and grown over.

As Colin tramped briskly along, he thought again of Etta. She had "dreamed" several times before, and each time, he had woken before his parents, soothed her back to sleep, and hidden her sin from the family. This morning he wouldn't be there. Suppose she were to blurt out her fantasy of strange creatures at the breakfast table? It was possible; she was young and naïve, and sometimes he worried that she didn't really understand how dangerous it was to speak of "dreams". Would Mother and Father report her to the Elders? Or would they, as he had done, try to hide her sinfulness?

He hesitated in mid-stride. Reluctantly he wondered if he should go back to protect her from any possible discovery. But if he did that, he would miss the opportunity of salvage at the cove, the possibility of adventure—something he had never experienced as the obedient son of Fergus, tending the sheep. *I'm almost sixteen*, he told himself. *It's important to show I'm a man, independent, worthy of supporting a wife.* By now the sun was well above the horizon, and everyone would be awake. He told himself that Etta was almost eight years old—old enough to know the danger of blurting out the story of her "dream".

He set off again along the track that finally reached the western cliff and wound along its eroded edge. From afar the sea had been a wrinkled grey pewter. Now he could see the waves still heaving restlessly, dashing themselves in fountains of spume against the dark rocks below. Though the wind itself had died, the sea had not forgotten the night's storm.

He struck off northwards until he came to the place where a track zigzagged from the cliff top down to the cove below. Even from this dizzy height he could see a fine harvest of timber cast up among the tangle of black seaweed along the foreshore, and he laughed out loud. How envied he would be! He began to pick his way carefully down the precipitous path. It veered to and fro, now clinging to the rockface, now hanging dizzily above the hungry sea and rocks below, with nothing but the tenacious roots of heath and gorse to hold the crumbling edge in place.

Colin was halfway down before his eye caught a movement among the tangle of timber and seaweed, a pale shape among the dark wrack. He stopped to stare, his heart pounding with excitement. *A beached seal!* What good fortune that would be! He could kill it with his knife, tie it with the rope he had brought with him, and haul it home. A seal would be far richer salvage than timber, and he would indeed find favour with Gwynne and her grandfather, the Elder Fisher Marlin. A seal meant good meat, as well as fur for clothing and oil for the winter lamps. Even its bones and flippers would be cleaned and dried to fashion spoons, buttons, and haircombs. Nothing of it would be wasted.

Already in his mind's eye he could see himself dragging his prize back to Merton before the awed eyes of the townsfolk. He broke into a jog, going as fast as he dared, as the path turned and doubled back beneath his feet. He panted and the sweat ran down his face, but he ignored it and ran on. The beach, which higher up had lain before him like a map, was now no longer visible, but was hidden by boulders and the low clumps of golden gorse that were just beginning to burst into honey-scented blossom.

The path flattened at last, giving way to a ridge of water-rounded pebbles, black and grey, beyond which lay the expanse of white sand smoothed by the outgoing tide. He ran eagerly across it, feeling it suck wetly at his shoes, to where he thought he had seen the seal.

The swirling movement of tide and storm into the rounded cove had deposited a single untidy pile of debris on the middle of the beach, halfway between the jagged headlands. Ships' timbers, broken lobster pots, a trail of tarred and torn netting, all of it enmeshed and festooned with the ribbons and blisters of seaweed.

Colin ran towards the pile, then stopped suddenly, his heart pounding, his breath coming in gasps. He blinked and stared. Lying on the sand, pale in contrast to the black seaweed that almost covered it, was no seal, but a white human hand. The body of some unfortunate sailor, he supposed, washed overboard in last night's storm. He swallowed his disappointment.

The vision in his head of his triumphant return had been so clear, as if it had actually happened.

He hesitated and then took a cautious step closer. Something was very strange here. The hand lying in the tangle of seaweed was as white as new wool, almost as small as Etta's, and—now he could see— there was an ornate silver ring on the middle finger, a ring finer than any worn by the women of Ariban. This was no sailor's corpse, but the body of a woman.

He swallowed sudden nausea, and the sweat sprang out again on his forehead. He had seen drowned men before, cast up on the shore near Merton Harbour, their faces bloated by the water, features obliterated by hungry sea creatures. But he had never seen a drowned woman. He shuddered. A horrid enough sight when one was surrounded by father and friends. But to find it alone . . .

In a surge of panic he wanted to run, to scramble up the steep path to the cliff top, to pretend he had never been here. Though the tide was now out, and the beach a wide expanse of wet-shining sand, by midafternoon it would be high again—a new moon high tide. The sea that had brought the corpse in might well take her back again, drawing her down into its depths among the wrecks of sunken ships, unknown. No one would ever know what he had seen . . .

While he hesitated, not daring to go closer but not retreating either, his eyes fixed in horror on that outflung white hand, he saw the fingers slowly curl and uncurl. There followed a kind of shiver of the body beneath the blanket of seaweed that covered it.

Colin's heart lurched. Had her hand really moved

of itself, or was it some sort of death spasm? The fingers curled again. He dropped his coil of rope onto the sand, ran across the beach, and began to tear at the tough seaweed, tossing it aside, pulling at the timbers that, only a short while ago, would have made him rejoice in the knowledge that his family would be the most envied in Merton Town.

At the base of the pile was an enormous tree bole, its roots tangled and twisted like a giant's hair. The woman was lying on her side, her body curved around its curve. Her hair was as tangled as the tree roots, caked with sand and weed, matted by seawater. One white arm was flung back; the other encircled a small chest, beautifully carved, bound with bands of brass, and with hinges and lock of the same bright metal.

Colin stared, his heart pounding, as another shudder ran through her body. He stared, as he would never have stared at a conscious woman. Her slim body was clad in a robe of some smooth fabric, thinner than wool and ornamented with bright embroideries, as if a cluster of spring flowers had fallen upon it. How beautiful it looked. But how strange. Then he realized, with the biggest shock of all, that this was no Ariban woman, but a foreigner!

And no foreigner was allowed on Ariban. That had always been the rule. Colin's mind raced. *What will the Elders say? Will they blame me for finding her? Should I leave her here to drown on the next tide? No, I can't do that. That would be murder.* His mind unaccountably jumped to his memory of the doomed dreamer, Alan. *But what has that to do with it?* He shook his head to clear it and forced his practical mind to work again.

Even though she had survived the sea, she would likely freeze to death, half naked on the wet sand, unless he were able to warm her. What should he do? He must haul her to the top of the beach, where the rocks would be dry. He must cover her with his jerkin and then make a big fire. In that order.

When he tried to lift her, he found that her body seemed to be wedged between the tree bole and the wooden chest. He moved her arm from the chest and bent to pick it up by the brass handles at each end. It wasn't until he had tugged mightily at it that he realized that the box had been tied securely to a wide piece of timber with leather thongs, and that other thongs bound the Stranger to the same timber. It was not just by luck that she had been washed ashore. She had been cast afloat on a crude raft from some foundering ship. She and the wooden chest. *How strange! To somebody, she—and it—must have been precious indeed.*

He wasted no time on this puzzle, but quickly cut the sodden leather strips with his knife and lifted the box. It was heavy for its size, and he wondered what it might contain. Treasure, perhaps . . . gold coins and jewels. Something important enough for careful hands to take the time to tie it to the raft alongside the young woman.

He dumped the box at the top of the beach and went back for the Stranger. Released from her bonds, she was light enough—not a woman, he realized now, but a girl perhaps a little older than himself—

and he had little difficulty in carrying her up the wet sand and laying her gently on a smooth dry rock. He stared down at her, his breath coming shakily. He had never held a woman in his arms before—not even Gwynne—and it was a very strange feeling. How delicate she looked, with white limbs and tiny waist, the damp garment clinging to her shape.

Fire, he reminded himself, and dragged together a pile of dry wood that had been swept above the last high-tide mark. Tinder-dry seaweed made a good starter, and with the flint and steel stored in his breeches pocket he soon got a splendid fire going, though he felt guilty in the making of it. To be burning wood was a terrible waste. On the island of Ariban wood was used only for repairing doors and shutters and for making furniture. Everything else was fashioned of stone, for Ariban was an island without trees but with plenty of rock. Wood was never burned.

Colin reminded himself that there was no dry peat closer than the village of Lynn, and peat would never give off the tremendous heat that timber did. He found himself amazed and almost afraid of the fierce and roaring flames.

He stood, his hand shielding his face, and watched the flames flicker green and blue through the salt-soaked wood, bemused by their savage power. Then he remembered his jerkin, hastily unlaced it, and laid it over her body. What else should he do? Recalling the treatment that the old wives had for near-drowned men, he reached out a hand and touched the smooth skin of her arm. He could feel his flesh burn hot against the chill of her body and forced himself to do what must be done: to rub her arms and legs. From the extremities towards the heart, that was the way, he remembered.

He rubbed vigorously until, little by little, his hands felt a responding glow replace the ice in her limbs. She moaned; her eyelids fluttered and then suddenly were open, and her eyes were staring at him, a deep and startling blue. He snatched his hands away, feeling his face grow hot, not knowing what to say.

Then he saw her hand fumble at the bare rock beside her and stammered, "You . . . you're quite safe. And . . . and your box too."

She struggled up on one elbow. "Where is it?"

He set it down close beside her. Her hand caressed the bands and, as she leaned towards the box, a leather thong around her neck swung forward, disclosing a brass key. Again he was aware of the shape of her body, so slender and finely made, beneath the damp gown. He snatched his eyes away and filled the silence with a joke.

"It's heavy enough. What does it hold? Gold and jewels?"

Then he bit his lip, thinking that she might be afraid that he would take it from her and leave her here for the next sea to wash away.

But there was no fear in her eyes. Only a glow of pride.

"Treasure far richer than either of those," she said innocently, as if she trusted him. *Treasure*, he thought, and part of his mind saw him presenting the box proudly to the Elders. Meanwhile the rest of his mind was crowded with questions.

"Who are you? What is your name and where do you come from? How came you to be tied to that raft?" The questions came tumbling out, but either she did not understand them or considered such questioning to be bad manners, for she said nothing.

Colin felt suddenly shy and turned to throw another piece of wood on the fire. As it blazed up, she reached out her hands towards it. "Oh, it is good to be warm again," she sighed.

Suddenly remembering the meal he had brought with him, he wondered if the Stranger was hungry. He untied the bundle from his belt and put the bread and cheese on the rock between them. He tore the loaf apart and offered her half. When she shook her head, he broke off a small crumb and tried to make her eat it, holding it to her lips. But she turned her head away, lay back on the warm stones, and closed her eyes.

He ate half of the bread and cheese, staring at her openly, now that she no longer looked at him. She was beautiful, in a way very different from the women of Ariban, different indeed from Gwynne. For an instant his mind toyed with the image of *this* woman sitting across from him at the table in his own house. Cooking his dinner. Weaving blankets for their bed.

Then he shook his head. *What nonsense! Why, I'm almost as foolish as Etta, with her dangerous dreams.* He forced his mind back to the reality of what he had done. He had saved a Stranger from the sea and brought a load of trouble down on his shoulders.

What was to become of her? Strangers were not allowed on the Isle of Ariban. Even the traders who came in the summertime were forced to moor out in the bay, while only the Elders of Merton Town and Lynn-by-the-Lake were permitted to go aboard and bargain with them for nails and iron pots, and so on, in exchange for the woollen goods for which the island was famous.

As far as Colin knew, a foreigner had never before been washed up on these shores. What would the Elders say? He was certain that they would not welcome her into the community. And would *he* be blamed for having saved her from the sea? Well, it was too late to worry about that now. She was alive, and he could hardly throw her back.

Her eyelids fluttered again. He said firmly, "You should eat. It will give you strength."

"I cannot," she whispered, her voice very weak. Her accent was not that of Ariban. *Foreign.*

"If you don't eat, you won't have the strength to walk, and I certainly can't carry you all the way up to the cliff top and back to Merton Town," he argued practically. Her strange eyes opened, looked blankly at him, and closed again. He sighed impatiently. "Then I'll have to go for help. You do understand that, don't you? You'll be safe here at the top of the beach. The tide won't reach this high. Don't move away from the fire. I'll be back as soon as I can get help. Do you understand?"

She nodded silently.

"Well, then." He stood up and was about to leave when his eyes fell on the coil of rope that he had dropped to the sand when he'd first seen the girl move. At least he could go home with something other than a half-drowned foreigner to show for his morning's work.

If he were to take a full load of wood with him, perhaps his parents would be less inclined to blame him for his interference. Swiftly he made a bundle of the soundest timbers he could find and bound them securely. Slinging the load across his shoulders, he toiled up the slow zigzags to the top of the cliff, the burden so heavy that he had to bend almost double to prevent it from dragging him backwards over the edge and down onto the rocks below. Certainly he could never have managed to carry the girl even this far, much less all the way back to Merton Town.

At the top he gave one last look down into the cove. He could just see the Stranger, a pale shape against the darker rocks, lying by the fire. Then he set off briskly homeward as fast as his load would let him, teased by his unanswered questions. Where could she have come from, this strange woman, in her fancy embroidered gown—so useless for working in—and with the grand silver ring on her finger? What had happened to the ship she was on? Sunk? Or sailing to some foreign port after abandoning her to the waves? Had she been fastened to the raft because she was someone precious, someone important?

There was a danger in even thinking these questions, he realized. They opened up a window onto a world other than Ariban. The Elders would certainly not approve of the way in which pictures flashed unbidden into his mind—pictures of other places, other ways. These thoughts were almost as bad as dreams. Not the thoughts of a grown man about to be wed at Midsummer, he told himself firmly.

Pushing these pictures out of his head, Colin grimly plodded on. He had reached Merton Town's grazing grounds before he met two shepherds, Craig and Blair. Thankfully, he eased the load from his shoulders and explained what they must do.

"A foreigner?" Craig repeated. "That'll be bad luck, won't it now?"

"Just a girl," Colin pleaded. "What harm can a girl cause? We can't leave her on the beach to die of hunger and thirst."

They looked at each other doubtfully. They were men like Colin's father, bearded and ruddy-faced from being out in all weathers. "I'm going now to tell my father," Colin went on rashly. "I'm sure he and my mother will be pleased to take her in. And my father will inform the Elders, of course."

"Ah, well then. So long as the blame is not on us." They nodded to each other and set off briskly towards Half-Moon Cove.

With a sigh of relief Colin swung his load back onto his shoulders and headed for home. Once there he threw open the door and dropped his load with a crash on the threshold. "Look what I've brought you, Mother," he began cheerfully, and then his voice trailed off. Hedda was sitting silently at the spinning wheel, while Etta stirred the stew bubbling on the peat fire, her head bent over so that her hair fell across her face. As she looked up, he saw her eyes, swollen with tears. Then he noticed the grim line of his mother's lips.

His heart plunged. *She's been found out*, he thought, and babbled on, his voice sounding falsely bright in the gloom. "I've the rights to as many more loads as I can carry in the next seven days. That big storm brought us a great gift. But more than that, much more . . ." He paused dramatically, waiting for their questions.

His mother's foot did not falter on the treadle, nor did her nimble fingers cease from pulling the wool off its smooth roll. "Pile the wood outside," was all she said. Not even a word of praise, which was surely his due. But her tone brooked no argument, and he did as he was told.

He came back into the house, coiling the rope. "It's almost noon. Where's Father?" *Surely Father will acknowledge the importance of my salvage*, thought Colin.

Hedda's lips tightened. Her foot paused, and her hand automatically went out to stop the wheel's spin. "Perhaps by now he's talking to Elder Shepherd. You'll know what about, I reckon."

"I?" Colin outstared her, trying to keep the guilt from his eyes and voice. "And why would I? Haven't I been away since before sunup, laying a claim to all the gifts of last night's storm?"

But she stared him down, as she had always been able to do. "You know full well what I mean, son. You've shared your sister's wicked thoughts, have you not? And encouraged them, perhaps."

"I have not," he burst out. "I've told her time and

again there's no such things as dreams. Nor such creatures as great beasts with teeth. I've tried and—" He stopped suddenly, realizing that he'd fallen into a trap, that he'd strengthened any case they might have against Etta, as well as implicating himself in hiding her wickedness from the family. And from the Elders.

He tried another tack, pleading, "She's only little, Mother. She'll grow out of it. Surely Father need not report her to Elder Shepherd?"

"And have him find out from Etta's friends that she's a sinner? Thank you very much for your advice." She spun the wheel again and caught the rhythm of the treadle's movement with a sure foot.

"What'll Elder Shepherd do, Mother?" he whispered, glancing sideways at Etta, who was drooping silently over the fire and the cook pot.

Hedda bit her lip and shrugged. "Who knows? Beat the wickedness out of her, I suppose."

Colin swallowed. "She's so little, Mother. She means no harm."

"No harm!" his mother hissed. "Trouble upon trouble, I prophesy."

Etta began to sob again.

Desperately Colin tried to think of a diversion and at once remembered what all the talk of the Elders had put clean out of his head. "Mother, Etta, you'll never believe what I found in Half-Moon Cove!"

"A fine load of timber. You already showed me."

"More than that! A *girl*."

"Some chit from Lynn-by-the-Lake, I suppose, gathering dulse out of season. And by herself? The hussy! But why wouldn't I believe that?"

"Because it wasn't anyone from Ariban, but a Stranger. About my age, I would guess. She must have been washed ashore in the storm."

The wheel stopped again, Mother's hand tight on its rim. She glared at Colin. "Not you too!" she snapped. "You'll be telling me in a moment that it's a mermaid you found on the shore. To have one storyteller in the family is disgrace enough. But two . . ."

"It's not a story, Mother. It's true, I swear. And no mermaid, but a real live girl. Well, you'll see for yourself soon enough. She was too weak to walk and I couldn't carry her up the cliff path, so I came back for help and luckily met Craig and Blair on the grazing grounds. They've gone to fetch her from the cove. She can stay here, can't she, Mother, until the Elders decide what to do with her? After all, I found her. She's salvage too, in a way. She can be useful to you, another pair of hands to milk and cut peat and draw water, so you'll have more time for spinning and weaving." He babbled on eagerly, pushing from his mind the memory of the delicate white hands and slender feet of the Stranger.

Hedda glared at him, her lips tight together. Abruptly she got to her feet, and Colin drew back, afraid for a moment that she was about to box his ears. "With my own eyes I must see this. Etta, watch that the stew doesn't burn. Come, Colin. We will go together to prove your truth or your lie." She yanked open the door and strode out, not waiting for him to follow her.

She was a strong island woman, his mother, and she walked at a steady pace that effortlessly ate up the distance from the town to the grazing grounds above, wasting no breath on idle chatter.

Keeping up with her, stride for stride, Colin eventually broke the silence. "What *has* Etta done?"

She gave him a sidelong glance. "You know full well, son. Did she not tell you in the night? Stories of fire-breathing beasts! Where did they come from, I ask you? Did she invent them out of her own wickedness? Or perhaps someone else has filled her head with lies?" She glared at him.

"Not . . . not I, Mother. And no one else, I'm certain," Colin stammered. "But she's still a child. Perhaps some children *do* have dreams until they're taught differently."

"Such talk! Shut your mouth!" She strode on silently for a while and then suddenly stopped and caught his arm. "Tell me the truth, son. Do *you* remember dreaming?"

Colin thought hard. Normally he fell asleep as soon as he crawled under his wool-filled quilt and knew nothing until the dawn light, peeking through a crack in the shutter, wakened him, bringing the rhythm of another day just like the one that had gone before it. But sometimes, though not very often, as he shook himself awake and felt the shock of the cold floor against his feet, there was a faint memory of—*something*. As if, between the sleeping and the waking, there had been a space. But filled with what? He pushed the vague memory away and shook his head. "No, I remember nothing."

She nodded. "There, you see. And that is how it should be. The world is right here and now and nowhere else, here on the Isle of Ariban. Birthing, growing, marrying, dying. Spinning and weaving. Fishing and shepherding. That is the whole of it, neither more nor less."

Colin had heard words like this since he was old enough to remember. They were the verbal framework that bound together and made sense of life. But suddenly the words seemed to take on a different shape. Instead of being a frame for this life of his, they were more like a sheep pen—bars, holding him back. But from what? What else *could* there be to life beside spinning and weaving, fishing and shepherding?

Again he found himself wondering where the Stranger had actually come from. Not from Ariban, that was certain. But what was life like on "Not-Ariban"? That was a question that had never teased his mind before. All he knew of Not-Ariban was the merchant ships that, twice or thrice a year, sailed into Merton Harbour, anchoring there and trading iron pots and nails and shearing clippers for dried fish and seaweed, for knitted sweaters and woven blankets.

Even though the Elders alone were permitted on board and the sailors were forbidden to step ashore even for a single night's revelry, the youngsters watched and wondered. Colin could remember hiding with the other children behind barrels, climbing on top of the fish-drying frames, staring at the foreigners. Their clothes were bright and as variegated as a puffin's feathers. Their hair was long, tied back in pigtails, and their voices were loud, given to much swearing.

The children didn't know the meaning of the strange words, but they knew not to repeat them, since anyone who was foolish enough to do so would have his mouth washed out with soap.

The foreigners, with feet that were bare and leather-hard, stomped about the decks of their huge wooden ships and shinned nimbly up the rigging. For these were big three-masted ships, not like the little square-sailed boats used by the fisherfolk of Ariban.

Colin suddenly remembered, as if it were yesterday, the wonder of being small, of holding the bright image of the foreign sailors secretly in his mind. Never talking about them. Any word or question would be answered with a frown or a slap.

He'd almost forgotten about those days, busy growing up, helping his father with the sheep and goats. The merchant ships still filled the harbour twice or thrice a year, but that was the Elders' business, none of his.

Recalling those childish pranks, Colin realized that he had never seen a foreign *woman*, not until today. It was hard to imagine that the pale creature, washed up among the jetsam of Half-Moon Cove, could be in any way related to those coarse red-faced sailors. The only things they had in common were the brilliant blue of their eyes and the darkness of their hair.

"Look, Mother." Colin pointed. "Now you can see for yourself that I wasn't lying."

Hedda shaded her eyes with her hand, for the sun was dazzling on the western sea, and the figures approaching them were only dark shapes. She stood, arms folded, waiting for them to come closer.

Without waiting for permission, Colin took off along the track, bounding from tussock to tussock to meet the shepherds. Craig and Blair had slipped two straight timbers through the armholes of their sheepskin jerkins and laced them together, and on this rough litter the Stranger lay unmoving. For a heart-stopping moment he thought she might be dead, she was so still, her eyelashes dark crescents against her white cheeks. But then he saw the gentle rise and fall of her breast and realized that she was only sleeping.

He stared in fascination, taking in the hair, as dark as that of the foreign sailors, and her dress, which had dried to show a lacy edge and many tiny pleats as well as the flowers he had already noticed. The fabric was finer and fancier than any he had seen before, and he wondered what his mother would make of it—and of the Stranger.

The shepherds had slung their satchels across their shoulders so as to free their hands for their load. Neither of them carried the small box, and it was not on the litter with the girl. Yet she had clung to it so fiercely.

He opened his mouth to ask the men what they had done with it, and then closed it again. If they had not noticed it, then it was *his* secret.

It must be back in the cove, he gloated. *And I have the salvage rights. The box is truly mine.* He waved a hand towards Hedda, watching away off, her arms folded across her chest. "My mother is waiting for you. She'll take the Stranger in," he promised, trusting in his mother's compassion once she saw the still small figure on the stretcher.

Then he was off, continuing his wild race across the pasture towards Half-Moon Cove. For the second time on this memorable day he zigzagged down the path, reining in his impatient strides to a safer jog trot. Soon the treasure chest would be his, with all it contained. *Not gold or jewels*, she had said. *Treasure far richer*. And it was *his* by right of salvage. He wondered what could possibly be more precious than gold or jewels. Pearls, perhaps? Or amber?

The cove was brilliant in the afternoon sunshine. He looked quickly around, his heart pounding with exertion. The pile of wrack lay where he had torn it apart. There were the cut lengths of leather thong that had lashed the chest to the raft. The incoming tide swirled about his ankles, washing at the makeshift craft. He ran to the top of the beach.

Among the dry pebbles, well above the high-water mark, were the remains of the fire he had lit. Ash and broken charcoal. Of the chest there was no sign. It was as if it had sprouted wings and flown away. *But it has to be here. It's mine.*

He turned around again and again, peering into a patch of shade, snatching at a tangle of seaweed. It couldn't have floated away, been washed out to sea. He stood bewildered, then slowly realized, with a growing anger, that he had been tricked. The Stranger had hidden her treasure chest. Pretending to be too weak to eat, even to raise her head, she had tricked him.

As soon as he had gone, she must have concealed it somewhere nearby. Under a pile of dry seaweed, behind a boulder. How dare she cheat him so when he'd saved her from drowning? Growing angrier with every failure, he overturned stones, tore apart clumps of seaweed, tossed aside sea-sodden timbers. The box was in none of these hiding places.

Maybe in a niche in the rock? In a cave? Would she have been clever enough to have found one? He looked up at the sun. It was long past noon, the afternoon half spent. *No time to search now.* His mother would expect him home. There would be more questions. Questions he did not want to have to answer. Somehow the ownership of the chest had become personal.

It's mine. I'm entitled, he argued silently. But until he actually held it in his own hands again, he could not lay full claim to it. *Strange and foreign. Far richer than gold or jewels.* His heart pounded at the thought, and he pushed aside the inner voice that told him, "It's not yours, Colin. It belongs to the Elders. To Ariban."

He glanced at the sun again, then quickly gathered another bundle of wood to haul back home. He needed some explanation of where he had been and what he had been doing.

But I'm not finished. Tomorrow or the next day I'll come back and find the chest, he promised himself. *The Stranger won't make a fool of me twice.*

CHAPTER TWO

By the time Colin reached Merton Town with his timber, the sun was low in the west, the pale new moon hanging in the sky above it. He slung the load onto the pile already stacked in the lean-to outside the cottage, clattering it noisily to announce his arrival, and pushed the door open.

"That was a fine salvage, son." Fergus smiled, a rare smile that seldom lit up his dour face. "Well done."

"Thank you, Father." Colin gloated secretly at the thought of the treasure box still hidden in Half-Moon Cove. *Just wait till Father sees that*, he told himself. Then his eyes went to the foreigner, seated in the fireplace nook, supping hungrily from a bowl of the stew Mother had prepared for their supper. She was swathed in one of Mother's blankets, her finery drying on a line above the hearth. There was some colour in her cheeks now. *Even more beautiful*, he thought, then flushed and stirred up his anger at her.

Cheat, he thought and almost asked her right out, *Where did you hide the chest?* He bit back the question and told himself again, *It is mine by rights, and whatever it contains, even if I must give it up to the Elders afterwards.* He knew that anything out of the ordinary, like jewels or gold, would certainly be deemed the property of the whole island, to be shared out fairly so that there would be no jealousy between families. But for now, before he turned it over to the Elders, he wanted to see it for himself, to touch the treasure with his own hands. What could *possibly* be richer than gold and precious stones?

Whatever it is, it is my secret, he thought, and realized guiltily that he had never had a real secret before. He had never had anything that was strictly his alone. Except for the secret of Etta's dreams, of course, he remembered soberly. The arrival of the Stranger and the mysterious box had made him forget all about Etta's calamity. *What's going to happen to her?* he thought with dread.

He was still thinking of Etta when the door was flung open, striking him on the shoulder. He turned angrily and then stood, his mouth open, his cheeks reddening. It was a rare occurrence, indeed, for both Elders to visit a home in the community. But here on the threshold stood Elder Fisher and Elder Shepherd. Each was clad in the homespun breeches and shirt worn by all the men of Merton Town, with the band of brown wool woven around the hem. In Elder Shepherd's hand was the official crook, and over his shoulders he wore the

Shepherd's band of fine white wool. Elder Fisher carried the gaff with the iron hook at its end, and around his neck was the necklace of shells. All these were emblems of their sacred office, handed down from generation to generation for as long as anyone could remember. From time to time the band might be mended or a broken shell replaced, but the ornaments themselves, and the crook and gaff, were as old as time.

Colin stood frozen, the pain in his shoulder forgotten, his heart pounding with the guilt of his two secrets, while Elder Shepherd's eyes seemed to skewer him to the doorpost.

"Well, Colin," the Elder snapped, "do you intend to gawk here all evening and let an old man stand outside?"

At the sound of his voice Hedda jumped to her feet. When she saw the insignia of the two men, the crook and the gaff, she curtsied deeply. "You are welcome to our house, Elders," she said formally. Colin could see a spark of fear in her eyes and his gaze shifted to his sister, standing, tear-stained, in the shadowy corner of the room. *What will they do to her?*

He backed unobtrusively away from the door and across the room until he was standing in front of Etta. He reached behind him and felt her hand grasp his tightly. *Two Elders. Why have both of them come about the small sin of a child's bad dream?*

Don't say anything, he wanted to warn his sister. *If they ask you about your "dreams", just shake your head and look blank*. But he could say nothing. All he could do was stand there helplessly and try to shield her from the Elders' piercing eyes.

To his surprise the Elders ignored them both. Elder Shepherd's pale blue eyes turned to Fergus and Hedda. "We are told that you are harbouring a foreigner under your roof. A Stranger to Ariban. A danger to our island."

Not Etta. He hasn't come here to punish Etta. Colin breathed a huge sigh of relief and stepped willingly forward. "I found her washed up in Half-Moon Cove, Elder. I went to salvage wood after last night's storm and there she was, lying in the midst of the seaweed like a—" He stopped. *Like a mermaid*, he had been about to say. *Why had Mother talked of mermaids? There are no such creatures. They are as sinful as dreams of monsters.*

"Like?" Elder Shepherd prompted.

"Like she was dead . . . like a dead seal," Colin quickly improvised. "That's what I thought she was at first, a seal washed up that I could salvage for Merton Town. Then I saw she was a girl and alive, so I pulled her from among the wrack and made a fire to warm her."

"Did she speak to you?"

"Not a word, Elder," he lied and looked warningly at her. She alone had not risen at the Elders' entrance, but continued to sit in the fireplace nook, her eyes downcast, a spoon in her hand, the bowl of stew in her lap. At Colin's words she glanced at him—a flash of those strange blue eyes—before looking down again.

Elder Shepherd drew in his breath with an audible hiss. Colin had the odd feeling that he was *afraid* of the Stranger, which was nonsense, of course. The Elders feared nobody. It was they who were to be feared.

"She comes from the sea, so she is my responsibility, Brother." Elder Fisher spoke to Elder Shepherd, who bowed in acknowledgement and stepped back silently into the shadows. "I will talk with her," he added harshly, and Hedda hastily moved a stool close to where the Stranger sat.

Elder Fisher settled himself and stared at her with a glare that must surely paralyse her with fear. "Young woman, do you know who I am?"

She looked at him frankly, her brilliant eyes unafraid. "Why, you must be the chief of this little village," she said in a clear, soft voice coloured with an accent that was foreign but charming.

But, still angry at her deception, Colin was in no mood to be charmed. *Little village! How rude and ignorant she is*, he thought, shocked. *Doesn't she know that Merton Town is the largest community on the Isle of Ariban? Over sixty families!*

Ignoring her insult, Elder Fisher went on, "I am one of the two Elders of Merton Town. With this gaff I guard and, if necessary, chastise the people. Do you understand?" He thumped the wooden end of the gaff on the stone floor so suddenly that Etta jumped and gave a stifled scream.

But the Stranger seemed not in the least bit awed. She continued to look calmly at Elder Fisher with those dark blue eyes. Colin found himself wondering if he had ever seen so intense a blue. A butterfly wing, perhaps. Or maybe the jewels in the hidden box might shine as brightly. But she had said they were *not* jewels. Of course, she might have said that only to mislead him so he wouldn't think the box important.

33

He brought his wandering attention back to Elder Fisher's interrogation. "What is your name, Stranger?"

"I am called Jennifer, which means 'white wave', and I am the daughter of Irvette and granddaughter of the great Godiva, who was the daughter of—"

The gaff pounded the floor again. "I am not interested in your lineage, child. Particularly through the female line, which can be of no significance. Who is your father, and where is he from?"

She shrugged, and the blanket slipped, showing a shoulder startlingly white against the tumble of dark hair. She pulled the blanket more closely around her. "His name is Ulric, but it is of no importance. In *our* clan the gifts come from our mothers."

"Ah. Now we come to it. What clan would that be?"

"The clan of Tellers."

"Tellers? That is an unfamiliar name. And what is the gift that comes only from the mothers? A glib tongue, I would guess, from the sound of yours."

She smiled, apparently quite unafraid. "You are partly right, Elder Fisher. A tongue is part of the gift. As well as memory and imagination. *We* are the storytellers."

"*Storytellers!*" Elder Fisher did not shout the hateful words. In fact his voice was almost a whisper. A shiver ran down Colin's spine. He began to wish fervently that he had not been so clever, that he had never gone to the cove, or that he had arrived much later, when the Stranger would have been dead and no bother to anyone. How much trouble had he stirred up in his innocent search for salvage?

As for this Jennifer, he told himself sternly, *there is no use in pitying her. She will probably be thrown back into the sea, and not from such an hospitable place as Half-Moon Cove, but from the top of South Peak, the highest cliff on the Isle of Ariban.* But he couldn't take his eyes from her—the proud tilt of her chin, the long slender neck, the incredible blue of her eyes. *Will the Elders really destroy such beauty?*

She still did not seem to understand the enormity of what she had just said. This was obvious from her calm face and gentle smile. Colin wondered if she was being stupid or deliberately wilful.

"Why, yes. We are all storytellers." She raised her dark eyebrows as if in surprise.

Keep quiet! Colin wanted to yell. *Stop condemning yourself with every word! You and your wicked storytelling tongue. You will get us all into trouble.* He clenched his fists till the nails dug into the palms of his calloused hands, willing her to be silent.

But she went on talking, her voice soft but clear, so that no word could be missed. "We carry in our memories the history of every family and clan in our land. Every deed, whether it be fair or foul, is committed to memory and becomes part of our saga."

"Ah, history." The Elder's voice was no longer edged with menace. "That is another matter entirely. Why did you not say so before?"

She looked up at him through her dark lashes. A sly, knowing look, Colin thought. "Why," she said softly, "what else would we tell?"

He drew a breath of relief. No fool, she had understood her danger and had slipped away from it like a fish from the gaff, like a sheep from the shepherd's crook.

"What, indeed?" Elder Fisher got slowly to his feet and turned to Elder Shepherd. "Brother, this family is a shepherd family and in your care. What say you? Are they worthy of the heavy responsibility of guarding this Stranger?"

Elder Shepherd inclined his head. "Fergus and his wife Hedda are indeed good members of the community. Their son is vigorous and hardworking. The daughter," he turned his piercing blue eyes to where Etta still lingered in the shadows, and Colin caught his breath in sudden fear, "is a child. Nothing ill is known of them."

Colin saw his mother, Hedda, put her hand on Fergus's arm, give him a small push forward. He could see the alarm in her eyes.

"F-forgive me, Elder Shepherd," Fergus stammered. We . . . we are only simple folk. To house a foreigner—a stranger to our shores—it is too much responsibility."

"Indeed," Hedda added eagerly, now that her husband had spoken up. "It is hardly fitting, Elder Shepherd. We have a growing son—"

"But he is already pledged to my granddaughter, Gwynne," interrupted Elder Fisher. "Surely you don't think he would be so fickle as to—?"

"Such a thought never crossed my mind," Hedda said hastily. In his mother's blush Colin detected her lie and was irritated by her belief that he might not be faithful to Gwynne. "Only—" his mother went on.

Elder Fisher chopped the air with the hand that

held the gaff, cutting off her objection. "When a fisherman lowers his net, he must be prepared to haul in the catch. Your son snatched this Stranger from the sea, and the responsibility for his action is yours."

"By your leave, sirs . . ." At the authority in the quiet words, they all turned to stare at the slight blanket-wrapped figure by the fire. "I am deeply grateful for my rescue, but there must be no question of my staying. Pray, let me take sail on the next vessel leaving your island. There need be no argument over responsibility, and I will trouble you no longer."

In the silence that followed her words, Colin felt suddenly as if the sun had slid behind a cloud. *She mustn't leave before I have a chance to get to know her, to hear her history, to see those dark blue eyes across our table.* He pushed these feelings aside. *She cheated me of the box,* he told himself. *Why should I want to see her? And I am promised to Gwynne. Why do I care what happens to Jennifer? Let her leave if she wants to.*

Elder Fisher strode across the kitchen until he was standing above the Stranger. "Where are you from that you do not know the ways of Ariban? That we allow no foreign ships into our harbour, save at Midsummer? No," he raised his hand as Jennifer began to speak, "I do not want to know what you call your land. To us it is only Not-Ariban. I forbid you to talk of your past or to spread lies about the ways in which your land and lives differ from ours. You will be silent. Do you understand?"

"I do, sir." Jennifer's voice was as cold as a winter wind, Colin thought. "May I ask you one question?"

"You may, though I do not promise to answer it."

"Of what are you afraid, sir?"

The gaff banged on the stone floor, and Colin jumped. *Be quiet!* he wanted to shout at her. *Be quiet before you get us all into trouble.*

But it was all right. The Elder's voice was calm as he answered the impertinent question. "We fear nothing, except contamination from the lies of foreigners."

She bowed her head. "Thank you, sir."

Elder Fisher grunted an acknowledgement and turned to his fellow Elder. "If you agree, Brother, I will pronounce: Jennifer, daughter of Ulric, you may stay on the Isle of Ariban, living in our ways, obeying our laws, working as we work, until the foreign ships come again to Merton Harbour after the full moon of Midsummer. Then we, the Elders of Merton Town, will decide whether you should go or stay."

"I thank you for your hospitality, sirs." Jennifer inclined her head with as much dignity as if she were an elder herself, Colin thought. Obviously, swathed in a blanket as she was, she could not rise to honour the Elders, but Colin felt uncomfortably that she was acting as if she were their equal.

However, Elder Fisher must not have come to the same conclusion, since he allowed a pale smile to flit across his face before turning and sweeping from the cottage, followed by Elder Shepherd. Nothing had been said about Etta's transgression. Had Father deliberately failed to report it, or had it been forgotten in the excitement of Jennifer's arrival? It seemed unlikely that the Elders would have decided to let the

Stranger live with them if they suspected Etta of wrong-doing. "Just a child," Elder Shepherd had said, and Colin had seen the relief sweep over his mother's face, washing away the lines of worry.

As the sun vanished behind the western cliffs, they sat down to a supper of stewed lamb and root vegetables, ladled out by Hedda from the iron pot that hung above the fire. *What a lucky day this has been*, Colin thought, mopping up the rich gravy with a hunk of bread: *a fine salvage, Etta saved from what had seemed like certain punishment, and now a "storyteller" to enhance the importance of our house.*

It had turned out amazingly well. Full of stew and emboldened by his luck, he looked across the table at the Stranger. "So tell us, Jennifer, how came you to be washed up on Ariban, bound to a raft?"

At his impertinence, Hedda hissed a warning and Fergus scowled silently. As for Jennifer, she smiled sweetly. "I believe I am bound to silence by the laws of your Elders. So my 'story' you will have to invent for yourself." *An answer to tease and irritate*, he thought.

It wasn't until they had gone to bed and the seal-oil lamps had been pinched out that Colin again remembered the little chest. *Later*, he thought sleepily. *When we're alone, I'll make her tell me where she hid it. Or maybe I'll find it for myself.*

39

Colin woke in the night and lay drowsily wondering what had disturbed him. The shutter of his window under the eaves was securely fastened, and tonight there was no storm wind to rattle the door and tear at the thatch. He had turned on his side, about to drift off to sleep again, when he heard the low murmur of voices from the other side of the heavy woollen blanket that separated his half of the attic from Etta's.

He was puzzled until he remembered that the Stranger, Jennifer, was sharing young Etta's bed. *Just girl talk*, he thought at first, uninterested. But then he realized that the soft monotone was not the rhythm of conversation, tossed to and fro like a ball of yarn; there were no pauses or interruptions, but a steady flow of narrative. It was more like . . . a story.

Perhaps the Stranger was telling Etta what she had not yet disclosed to anyone else: the history of where she had come from and the circumstances that had led to her being lashed to a spar and set adrift on the stormy waves, together with her treasure box. He threw aside his covers and crept silently across the floor to squat by the dividing curtain. Her voice, though clear, was very soft, and he had to strain his ears to catch the words.

". . . at that Princess Etta took the magic sword in her right hand and mounted her fearless steed. Holding her courage as steadily as her sword, she rode out of the castle, over the hill and down through the dale, across the river and through the wasteland, until at last she came to the cave of the arch-dragon, Pyros.

"All was dark and still within, and she was tempted to turn back, but she knew that, though she was sore afraid, it was only by overcoming her fear that she could overcome her enemy.

"'Come out, foul fiend, and prepare to do battle,' she cried as loudly as she could."

Colin crouched as close to the curtain as he could without being seen. This wasn't the history of the foreigner, but something even more strange. A *story*. And *Etta*, its heroine.

"From within the depths of the cave was a stirring and then a rattling and clattering, followed by a fiercesome snort. A gout of flame burst forth from the entrance to the cave, and Princess Etta's steed whinnied and drew back with a shiver. Etta dismounted, because she knew that her horse's fear of fire might distract her in the final struggle and that, in any case, the battle must be fought only between the dragon and herself.

"She slapped him lightly on the flank to send him away, and then she stood alone in front of the cave with the sword in her hand. As she stood there, terrified and trembling, a wondrous thing happened. She began to feel courage flowing from the blade of her magic sword into the haft and from the haft into her hand and so through her body to her heart.

"She cried out again in challenge, 'Come out, Pyros!' and stood firmly as, with more clatterings and clangings of its scales and with much snorting and flickerings of flame, the arch-dragon slowly unwound its coils and slithered out of the darkness of the cave to confront her.

"Oh, it was a great monster indeed, was Pyros, with scales of green and gold, each scale edged with sharp spines; its eyes were as ruddy as the western sun before a storm, and its great teeth were as white and jagged as the sea breaking on a rocky shore. As for its breath, it was as hot as a smithy's fire and as foul as rotting fish."

Colin shivered. *These are only words*, he told himself firmly. But in his mind grew a picture of the great dragon Pyros. As if it were really *there*. He ran his tongue over his dry lips and cautiously moved the curtain, the better to hear every word. The soft voice of the storyteller continued to weave its magic . . .

"But Princess Etta did not budge. She stood before the monster with legs as firm as the trunks of trees, and she held the sword steadily in front of her so that its steely tip pointed straight at the throat of Pyros. 'Begone, foul monster,' she shouted, 'and nevermore return to this island!'

"Behold, at her words, power flowed from her heart to her hand, from her hand to the pommel of the sword and so down the blade. And the arch-dragon Pyros began to dwindle. His colours faded to the greyness of dawn and soon his breath was no hotter than a peat fire at night. He shrank until he was the size of a sheep. And then to the size of a lamb. He dwindled until at last there wriggled on the ground in front of Princess Etta a worm no bigger than a horned caterpillar. Princess Etta sheathed her magic sword and she stepped upon the worm and ground it into the dirt under her heel.

"And what became of Princess Etta after she rid the island of the arch-dragon? Why, she rode back to the palace to go on with her life, doing the ordinary things that princesses, like other mortals, must do: chopping the vegetables and stirring the stew, carding the wool and learning to spin. But the magic sword she hung on the wall of her bedroom, knowing that if ever another monster dared to come to the Isle of Ariban, she would be able to vanquish it as she had overcome the arch-dragon Pyros."

"You mean it never came back?" Colin could just hear Etta's drowsy voice.

"Never. It was utterly destroyed under the foot of Princess Etta."

"Maybe another dragon would be angry and fly to Ariban to revenge the death of Pyros?"

"Indeed not. Dragons can never speak directly to each other, because their words are fiery and destroy everything in their way, even another dragon. But their minds are linked, so that as Pyros was dying he sent a message to all the dragons in the whole world, warning them to stay away from the Isle of Ariban and the deadly sword of Princess Etta."

"No dragons ever again?"

"Not ever."

"Hmm . . ."

At Etta's sleepy murmur, Colin cautiously straightened the curtain and crept, shivering, back to bed. As he huddled under his quilt, rubbing the warmth back into his cold feet, he was brimming with questions. Where had the stranger found this strange story? It wasn't true. It could never be true, could it? *Surely there are no such creatures as dragons*, he told himself. *And Etta is certainly no princess*. Why, Jennifer had told lie upon lie! Didn't she know that only what could be seen with the waking eye, or tasted or touched or smelled or heard, was real? Anything else was a lie. And lies were evil. Did this make Jennifer evil?

He puzzled over this until at last he fell asleep again, and was still asleep when his mother called him to the breakfast table. As he scrambled into his breeches and shirt, a memory of a dragon dream came back to him, a dream in which *he* had held a magic sword and killed a great monster. Just a faint echo, no more. He pushed it away. *Dreaming is wrong*, he told himself as he tied the string of his breeches. *Dreaming is a lie*, he told himself again as he climbed down the ladder into the kitchen. By the time his foot touched the stone floor, the monster-memory was gone.

"Sleepyhead," crowed his sister. "Jennifer and I have been awake for *ages*, haven't we, Jennifer?"

He blinked the sleepiness from his eyes and stared at Etta. She was like a new-made person this morning. Her cheeks were pink, and in her eyes was something he had not seen for a long time. He puzzled over it and realized that it was fearlessness. For almost as long as he could remember, Etta's eyes had been cast down, the expression in them hidden by her lashes. Like all the small children on Ariban, she was meek and quiet, the way children were *supposed* to be.

Colin felt a sudden twinge of anxiety. If Elder Shepherd should see her now, he would know that she was up to no good. That she was trouble. She bubbled like fermented berry juice.

"Why are you staring at me like that?" Etta's voice

broke into his thoughts. "It is Jennifer you should be looking at. Doesn't she look nice?"

Shyly he looked across the table. His mouth gaped and he blinked. He would hardly have recognized her. Her wild tangle of dark hair had been tamed into two tight braids and, instead of the flimsy foreign dress with its lacy edge and embroidery, she was wearing a blouse and skirt of his mother's, beige homespun with a border of darker wool. It made her look ordinary, and more grown-up, as if she were indeed full-grown. Only the fact that her head was not covered showed that she was still an unmarried woman.

"Doesn't she look nice?" Etta persisted.

"Yes, very nice," he said mechanically, though it wasn't true, he thought. She looked more ordinary, less foreign, far removed from the wild pale creature he had found tangled in the seaweed.

Then she raised her eyes and gave him a small smile, and in her eyes alone was a connection to the stranger he had rescued: that brilliant unnameable blue.

"Don't stand there like a stick, boy," Hedda scolded. "Eat your porridge and be off to help your father."

"What will Jennifer do today?" he asked between mouthfuls of gruel and goat's milk.

"Women's work. What is it to you?"

"I thought I could show her around Merton. Introduce her to people." *She's my discovery, after all*, he thought resentfully.

"People will meet her soon enough," his mother said drily. "They'll come by with this excuse or that to take a peek. No need for you to hang around." She almost pushed him out of the house as if she were eager to get rid of him.

Colin helped his father fashion a new shutter for Etta's window from a piece of salvaged wood and glimpsed Jennifer walking with Etta down to the well at Merton Town crossroads. Then he was sent to the uplands to cut grass for the goats, which were kept tethered close to the house.

On his return he spied Etta trying to teach Jennifer how to milk a goat. He was drawn by their laughter. He had never before heard Etta laugh like that. What was so funny? As he went closer, his father called to him to strengthen the fence around the vegetable plot with the smaller pieces of lumber he'd hauled from Half-Moon Cove.

The next day was as frustrating. It was his turn to watch the flock. From the grazing lands he saw two figures—one tall, one short—carry Hedda's loaves to the town oven for baking and, later, run back with the hot bread wrapped in cloths.

At mealtimes it seemed that Hedda's eyes were always on him, and at nighttime she sent Jennifer and Etta up to their attic bedroom, where they whispered and giggled together. Colin was set to whittling a new set of clothespins for his mother. He had never a moment alone with Jennifer. Not one.

It is not as if it were for myself, he argued. *I have to make sure she doesn't spread those lies of dragons and princesses among the young people of Merton Town. I have to warn her.* But how could he, when she and Etta were together day and night? It was almost as if Etta had discovered a sister and, in so doing, had forgotten her brother. *I am not jealous*, he told himself. *That would be foolish. It is just—inconvenient.*

It wasn't until after the dry morning service on Sunday—a reminder of do's and don'ts—that he finally caught her alone—alone, that was, in the midst of a crowd of young people enjoying their holiday.

Sunday was a day of rest, and in the fine spring weather, once the sermon was over, the young people had picnics of freshly baked rolls and cheese, of lamb pasties and cake filled with dried berries. Out in the upland meadow, the older children were free to walk or laze the afternoon away, while the younger ones played games of herding sheep or spinning wool.

"But no stories?" Jennifer stared in horror as Colin carefully explained that lies were sinful and that those who told them would likely be severely punished. "How can you live without stories?"

"Very well, as you can see," he snapped back, stung by her criticism. "Look at us—how well we do and how prosperous we are."

For a moment she was silent. Then she spoke slowly, as if searching for gentle unoffending words. "What I see, Colin, are dull, meek children playing games that are just an echo of the grown-up world. Pretending to herd sheep or nurse babies. Games played with no joy or imagination."

"And you would rather bring them up to believe in imaginary princesses slaying imaginary dragons? What wicked lies!"

"No, my stories are not that." She shook her head. "When I tell you a lie, that lie is the truth." It sounded like a quotation, part of something bigger. By itself it made no sense.

"That's stupid."

"No. It is the power of Story. Etta needed to be strong, to conquer her fear, so I made her into a princess and gave her a magic sword of courage to overcome her dream monsters. You were listening, weren't you? Surely you understood?"

"Understood? Why, dreams are lies too. They are wicked."

"I disagree. Sometimes they come to teach us how to live, how to behave."

He jumped to his feet. "No. They are always wrong. And made-up stories are wrong too." His voice rose, and some of the children playing nearby turned curiously to stare at him. He knelt beside Jennifer and whispered, "Etta was already in trouble before you arrived. Mother and Father were planning to report her to Elder Shepherd."

"What would he have done?"

Colin shook his head. "I don't know exactly. I never had dreams."

"You must have done. Everyone does. Only you cannot remember them."

"What do you mean?"

"I expect those Elders of yours have found ways of teaching you to forget your dreams and even forget the forgetting. Washed away, just as a beautiful drawing in the sand can be washed away by the tide."

He stared at her. "Why in the world would a person be so foolish as to draw in the sand? Of course the tide would wash it away. Anyway, whether we have forgotten or whether we never have dreamed isn't important. The dreams and the lies are gone, and that is good."

"Good? Why, it's terrible! A whole island of people without story, without imagination, without dreams? I don't know how you can bear to live this way."

He flushed angrily. "We have a good life here on Ariban. It is the best place in the whole world. You have no right to criticize us. I believe the Elders are right in not allowing us to talk to foreigners like you, if these are the crazy ideas you bring among us."

"Not talk to foreigners? What can you mean? The ships come into your harbour at Midsummer. Your Elders told me so."

"Not to *land*. You're the first Stranger who has ever been allowed to stay on Ariban. I can understand why the Elders made that rule. They were very wise. The way you think is just going to make trouble. And I will be blamed for it, since saving you from the sea was my doing."

"Would you rather have had me die? Perhaps you should have thrown me back like an unwanted fish!" Jennifer's blue eyes pierced Colin, and he felt himself blushing.

"Of course not," he stammered. "But if I hadn't found you—"

"Then I would be dead and you would be free of the blame. Oh, poor Colin!" she mocked him. "The worst they can do is send me packing on the next ship, and a good thing too, for you seem a sad and sorry lot. As for you, my poor Colin, they can just make you 'forget' I was here, as they must have made you forget your dreams when you were a child."

"You think you know so much, Stranger. You think they'll send you away?" Colin was stung by her calling him "poor Colin" as if he were a child, and he spoke roughly. "I've heard rumours of what is done to those who go against our ways. We have a saying: 'Tis easy to rid an island of evildoers when the cliffs are high and the sea below is angry."

"Murder?" She drew in her breath. Then she shook her head. "Whispers to frighten small children. No more!"

"I remember once—" he stopped. "Yes, I *do* remember. There was a young fisherman who had crazy dreams. He was touched by the moon, some said. I heard tell that they tied his hands behind him and chased him over the western cliff. From the top of South Peak, over there, see? If you don't forget your wicked stories, it might happen to you. And maybe to Etta and me as well."

She shivered and drew close around her shoulders the shawl that Hedda had lent her. "What an ugly place! How can you bear to live here?"

"But Ariban is beautiful. And good. Nobody goes hungry. Nobody has less than his neighbours. If a fisherman dies at sea, his widow and children are cared for."

"But you're all afraid."

"That's not—" Colin stopped, remembering the nights when he had slipped into Etta's room to quieten her, to conceal from their parents the shameful fact that she had been dreaming; remembering the look on his mother's face when Elder Fisher and Elder Shepherd had come to their house the other day, and the relief when Elder Shepherd had dismissed Etta as "only a child".

"We're not afraid for ourselves," he argued. "Only for Etta, because she's different."

"So everything on Ariban is beautiful so long as no one is different?"

"What's wrong with that? There have to be rules. Rules against lies, stories, dreams. Things that make people discontented."

"Things that make them *alive*. Oh, Colin, you will never understand, I can see that now. It is hopeless. I *must* leave. Will you help me escape?"

"Escape?" Colin stared at her stupidly.

She sighed impatiently. "I have no future here. I *am* a storyteller. It is what I do. There is no place for me on Ariban."

Escape? His anger at her faded. If she left, there would be—a space. An emptiness. He swallowed. "You don't have to go." The words tumbled out eagerly. "You can learn to weave and spin and knit like the other women. To keep the fire going and to cook. You can become like us."

"Ugh! Knit and weave? Let me tell you, in the time of our glory, we storytellers lived in palaces and castles and travelled to manors and inns across the breadth and length of the country. Our fame spread ahead of us, and everywhere we went we were made welcome and treated with honour. We were paid for our stories not just in food and shelter, but with gold and jewels."

"If you were so important, then why were you cast up alone on the shores of Ariban?"

"Because I *am* important—oh, not for myself—for what I carry. So when our ship foundered in the storm, the brave sailors bound me to a raft in the hope I might survive."

What I carry, she had said. *Gold and jewels!* He jumped up and stared down at her. Why, he had almost forgotten! "Is that what you have hidden in the little chest, gold and jewels?"

"What chest?" She looked at him with wide blue eyes so innocent that Colin wondered for a minute if indeed the box were real. His mouth opened and closed again. Had she bewitched him into imagining a box? No, of course it was real. He had held it and felt its weight. It *was* real, and she had hidden it. Now she was teasing him, as if he were a child.

Angrily he snapped, "Perhaps it would be best for us all if you *did* leave. But you know as well as I do that the merchant ships are not due till Midsummer. If the Elders want you to leave then, you will be free to go. If they choose for you to stay—though I cannot imagine that they will do that—then you will have to smuggle yourself aboard and pay for your passage . . . if you have gold enough in your non-existent box."

She laughed. "I have what is better than mere gold and more priceless than rubies. I have stories to tell."

Colin gave an exclamation of disgust. "You're hopeless!"

She laughed and jumped to her feet. "I know." She went over to where a group of young girls were playing "mother". "Children, I have a new game. May I share it with you?"

Colin stared after her, his hands doubling into fists. She was infuriating! And he was no closer than before to finding out where Jennifer had come from or where she had hidden the mysterious box; surely she was playing with him when she denied that it contained gold and jewels? *Trouble*, he thought angrily. *You are nothing but trouble.*

Already the children were eagerly playing the new game—a strange one in which they crept close to Jennifer, who stood with her back to them. Suddenly she would turn and the children had to stop still. Anyone she caught moving was out of the game. It seemed pointless to Colin, but the children were laughing and screaming with a fear that was partly pretend and partly real. Already the grown-ups were looking towards them, frowning. The Stranger was a disturber of peace and order, there was no doubt about it. Maybe he *should* tell Elder Shepherd all he knew about her.

But if he did that, he would have to disclose Etta's dreams. He thrust his hands into his pockets and swerved away from where the Elders sat together on the high ground . . . right into the path of Gwynne. She was, perhaps, the last person he wanted to see at that moment, when his mind was full of the tantalizing, irritating, *impossible* Jennifer.

CHAPTER THREE

"Colin, where have you been? I have been look-ing for you all afternoon." Gwynne smiled sweetly and her voice was soft, not accusing, but Colin felt himself flushing guiltily.

"Nowhere particular," he said vaguely.

"Your father has kept you so busy, I have seen nothing of you all week." She sighed dramatically. "And I suppose you have been too occupied looking after the Stranger to have any time left for me."

Colin tried to ignore the bite in her voice. "Well, Mother did say I should look after her," he excused himself automatically, and then bit his lip. Why should he lie to Gwynne, of all people? But could he tell her the truth? That his mind was occupied with the puzzle of the missing treasure box? That the newcomer was spinning stories for his innocent little sister? That he was afraid of what the Elders would do if they found out that he was concealing these things?

But if I tell her, she'll go straight to her grandfather, Elder Fisher. That's what she'll do, a warning voice spoke inside his head. *Anyway, it is more than just those worries. It's as if Jennifer has spun an invisible net around me. Am I bewitched?*

"Let us go for a walk," Gwynne suggested, and a little reluctantly he joined her, strolling towards the lower slopes of South Peak.

"This week I finished weaving my fourth blanket," Gwynne said.

"I'm sure it looks very fine," Colin answered absently, wondering when he could possibly get away and explore Half-Moon Cove more thoroughly. The box *must* be there.

"My bride chest is filled." Gwynne's voice was matter-of-fact. "So now we must ask your father for his help in building our house."

"I found a lot of good timber down at Half-Moon Cove after that last storm. Enough for doors and windowsills and shutters," Colin boasted.

"And you found the blue-eyed Stranger there as well." There was an edge to her voice, and he glanced at her as they climbed the grassy slope. *Is she jealous of Jennifer? But that is foolishness.* He noticed that her chin stuck out, rather like her grandfather's. It was an obstinate chin, he realized, one that indicated its owner was used to getting her own way. Her skin was dusted with freckles and her hazel eyes were set rather too close together for beauty.

Why have I never seen these things before? Colin

asked himself. And a shocking question flashed unbidden into his mind. *Do I really want to marry Gwynne?*

He told himself not to be foolish. What else could he do? His parents and Gwynne's had settled the matter when they were still children. He had grown up knowing he would marry Gwynne. That was the way important matters were ordered on Ariban. So why was he questioning it now?

It's all the fault of that blue-eyed Stranger, he thought angrily. *She's brought nothing but trouble. Jennifer—such an odd-sounding name. Jennifer . . .*

He began to walk faster, no longer talking to Gwynne, but scrambling up over rocks, pulling himself up the steeper places with handholds of stiff wiry heather, until he was far ahead of her. When he reached the peak he stood there, gulping air, feeling the wind blowing through his hair and cooling his sweaty forehead. There was something about the uplands and the sea beyond that made him feel unexpectedly free and happy. Buffeted by winds blown in from other distant lands, he felt almost as if he had escaped.

But escaped from what? he asked himself.

Gwynne's touch on his arm brought him back to reality with a start. The wind had tangled her normally smooth hair and brought colour to her cheeks. She looked almost pretty. Though not as beautiful as *her*.

Colin turned his back on the sea and looked down from their eagle's viewpoint at the people scattered across the meadowland below. In their plain clothes of beige and buff, cream and brown, they were hardly distinguishable from the wandering sheep, from whose fleece their clothing had come.

He found himself remembering the gaudy clothes of the sailors on the merchant ships, and Jennifer's dress embroidered with the colours of spring flowers. *They're just foreigners!* he told himself fiercely. *Our ways are right!*

"You must talk to your father," Gwynne said again. "We should get our house finished before Midsummer."

"Yes, of course." Colin nodded.

"Why don't you talk to him today, when he is not busy working?"

He felt as if those invisible bars were closing around him. He tried to wriggle free. "I have an errand to do first, Gwynne. There is still some good wood left in the cove. The storm came last Sunday night, so I have salvage rights for only one more day."

"Of course. Why don't I come with you?"

Colin's heart sank. How could he hunt for the treasure chest if she were there? He thought desperately of an excuse to go alone. "To go so far without a companion would not be proper," he said primly, and felt a secret glee at the sight of her vexed expression.

"You are quite right," she said. "But come back soon and talk to your father about our house."

"I won't be long," he promised, and set off at a run down the northern flank of South Peak. Cutting across country this way would save considerable time, though the going was rougher. But the physical exertion of bounding over tangled heather roots, pushing through stands of young bracken, feeling the sweat run down his chest, gave Colin a savage satisfaction that tamely following the regular trail could not have provided. He told himself that he wasn't running away from anything, but running *towards* it.

The tide was coming in and was about halfway up the beach as he stood at the foaming water's edge and looked around. *Where could she have hidden the little chest?* The cliffs that cupped the small cove were as full of cracks and holes as a loaf of bread. Even though he had been coming to this cove for as long as he could remember, he still did not know them all. She was a foreigner and had had little time in which to find the perfect hiding place.

Suppose I were the Stranger? The thought flashed through Colin's mind. It was an intriguing idea. He had never imagined in quite this way before, as if he were someone other than Colin, son of Fergus and Hedda. He scrambled across the water-polished pebbles to the top of the beach where he had made the fire. The dark mark still stained the stone where the timbers had burned.

He looked around, saying to himself, *I am a stranger with something precious to hide. Where would I put it? Bury it in the sand? Too shallow. Under the stones? Too easily seen.*

The afternoon sun reflected off the northern wall of the cliff at an angle that left the telltale shadows of cracks and niches. A dozen possibilities! He scrambled to his feet and ran across the pebbles. Some holes were too small, others a forearm or more deep.

Easy to plunge in his hand and test his theory. But he found nothing.

Frustrated, he stood and looked again along the cliff face. She couldn't have gone far, she had been too weak. Then it occurred to him that it was now late afternoon, while on that other day he had left her before noon, when the sun would have been shining almost straight down, marking the cliff with very different shadows. *I must come back in the morning and see the cove as she saw it*, he told himself. *I will find the treasure chest. I will! Not just for what it may contain but for what it is. A part of Jennifer. Something that she values.* It was almost as if having the chest would bring her closer to him.

He stopped at this strange thought and stared blankly at the beach. Then he remembered he had told Gwynne that he was going for wood. *And I haven't even a length of rope with me. What a fool I am!* He hesitated and then undid the cord that belted his shirt about his waist, using it to tie together a big enough bundle to allay suspicion.

As he trudged back to Merton with his load, Colin's mind lingered on the memory of the little box. Dark wood with designs carved both on the top and side panels, and with bands and hinges of brass. And a brass lock, well made and heavy. Not the sort that one could pry open with a knife. He stopped for breath and to wipe his forehead on his arm and, in a flash of memory, recalled *her* leaning forward, the small brass key between her breasts swinging forward on its leather thong. *I must get the key as well as find the box*, he told himself.

It was almost twilight, and people were returning to their cottages as he entered the town. Though nobody said anything, some of them looked at him askance. What was the matter now? Why, carrying a load of wood on a Sunday! He bit his lip. What a foolish mistake. One he would never have made before *she* came and drove the rules out of his head.

He left the load in the shed and caught Etta alone as she went to the town well for water. "I'll help you," he said.

She looked at him in surprise. "What's the matter, Colin? You never help me carry water anymore."

"So, I will today. Come on."

As they walked along, he said, "There's something you must do for me, Etta."

"Of course. Whatever I can." She beamed at him.

How well she looks, now that she's no longer consumed with fear and bullied by Hedda because of it, he thought. *She seems to have actually grown taller in the week that Jennifer has been with us. So I owe the Stranger that, at least.* For an instant he felt guilty at his sly plan to take her treasure chest, but he hardened his heart. *Jennifer is a foreigner and therefore not to be trusted*, he told himself. *And the box is mine by the laws of Ariban.*

"It's a big secret," he said to Etta, as he swung the pails, one after the other, down the well.

"I'll keep it. I promise."

"This is it, then. You know the key she wears around her neck. Does she take it off at night?"

"Of course. She slips it under her pillow. I asked her why she kept it there, and she laughed. She said that the key was a magic amulet, 'opening the gateway to a world of hidden joys and delights,' she said. Isn't that a funny thing to say about an old key? I asked her what it *really* opened, but she wouldn't say. She made a joke and told me another story. I *do* like her, don't you, Colin?"

"She told you another story? But Etta, you *know* stories are wrong. You know what will happen to you if the Elders find out you've been listening to stories," he whispered, as they began the return journey with the laden pails.

"I don't care." Etta pouted. "I love her. I wish she were my real sister."

"Etta, listen to me. You've got to take that key from under her pillow first thing in the morning, before she's awake."

"But why? I'm sure if I were to ask her, she would lend it to me."

"No. It must be done secretly. That key is bad. It will bring disgrace to our whole family if she is allowed to keep it."

"Now that *is* a story, Colin. That's very wrong of you. She is truly good. Why, she saved me from my bad dreams and now I don't have them anymore."

"Hush. Keep your voice down. Someone might overhear. Maybe she is good, but, I promise you, the key is bad."

"I don't think I should."

"Etta, you *promised*. Trust me. You must get me the key secretly. It's so simple. A hand under her pillow before she wakes in the morning."

"What'll I say when she finds out it's missing?"

"Tell her your brother has taken it to claim his salvage rights. She will know what I mean."

"Well . . ."

He held the door open and together they hauled in the full pails. "Not a word to anyone about this, mind," he whispered.

He awoke before dawn and lay listening to the rooster's crow until the blanket between their rooms moved and he saw Etta's hand through the gap. In an instant he was on his feet, taking the key from her, slipping the thong around his neck. Etta opened her mouth, and he put his finger over her lips. She nodded and tiptoed back to her bed.

Colin scrambled quickly into his clothes, climbed down the ladder to the kitchen below, eased the door open, and slid out into the grey morning mist. By the time Jennifer noticed that the key was missing, he would be on his way to the cove. Before long the chest would be in his hands and the treasure would be his to gloat over, even if only for the little while until he gave it to the Elders to distribute.

Mine for a small while, he repeated to himself. *I found it. I deserve that, don't I? Then it will belong to the Elders and to Ariban.* Far richer than gold, she had said. The words marched through his head in rhythm to his footsteps. *Far richer than jewels.*

His shadow danced ahead of him across the coarse

grass as the sun rose over the eastern ocean. He came to the cliff above the cove, his breath rough, his forehead sweaty despite the cool of the morning. Such a short time since the storm, since he had come to the cove and found *her*. And his whole life had changed in ways that still bewildered him. Once again his feet found their way between the stones and roots on the treacherous path down. Once more he stood on the pebbled shore and looked around. But now he was not looking for salvage, but for her treasure box. In which of the many crevices had she hidden it?

The telltale shadows darkened the cliff face, and he ran from one to another, plunging his hand into niches, ducking into small caves. *She will not beat me*, he promised himself, and searched on until, at last, he found her hiding place.

It had been cunningly chosen. Jennifer had rolled a stone in front of what was no more than a deep recess. A casual eye or hand would see no more than the stone, missing the treasure lying behind it.

Where did this strange foreign girl learn such a trick? he asked himself. Gwynne would not have thought of a ruse like that in a hundred years. He discovered it himself only because the stone had scraped the inside of the niche, leaving a paler mark.

Once he had pulled the stone out, he could see the box clearly, nestled into the rock as if the space had been made for it. He reached for it eagerly, clawing for a fingerhold on the latch and skinning his knuckles into the bargain. How heavy it was for so small a size. *Gold and jewels*, he told himself. *Or something even richer*.

He dropped the box onto the stony beach and knelt beside it, licking his sore knuckle. He lifted the thong from around his neck. The key slid smoothly into the lock and turned sweetly. For an instant he hesitated, tasting the moment of triumph that was within his grasp. Then he flipped back the two hasps that held the lid tight and slowly opened it, holding his breath, his eyes already imagining the glistening treasure.

So strong was this picture in his mind that the reality did not sink in for a heartbeat or two. Then, with a shout of anger, he upended the box, spilling its contents recklessly onto the beach.

Out tumbled a half-dozen books, strange small books, nothing like his mother's recipe book, or the folded charts the fisherfolk used, or even the Book of Rules from which the Elders read on Sundays. These were bound in leather, some of them tooled into extravagant patterns, others ornamented in bright colours. Two had tiny gilt hasps to hold the books closed, so that they resembled small jewel cases.

For an instant hope flared and he flicked open the hasps, opened the covers and shook the books by their hinges. Out fell a single picture that had come loose from its page. It glided on the breeze as a leaf might, and came to rest among the boulders at the top of the beach.

Automatically he reached out and retrieved it. It was a picture of a young man, staff in hand, standing upon a headland, gazing into the distance. He stood much as Colin had done the previous day on South Peak, when the bars of the prison that was to be his life on Ariban seemed to close around him.

He found himself leafing through the book to find the place from which the picture had fallen. It faced the beginning of a story, one of several that this small book contained. Almost without meaning to, Colin found himself trying to decipher the words. He knew how to read and even how to write a little. It was a boast on Ariban that none of its citizens was ignorant; but he had got out of practice, now that his few years of schooling were behind him. He squatted on a sun-warmed stone and, with a finger capturing each difficult word, he began, stumblingly, to read aloud.

"Once upon a time there was a young prince whose future was bound in duty: duty to his father, the king; duty to the land he must one day inherit and rule wisely; duty to the daughter of the neighbouring princedom, whom he must one day marry.

"'Before these burdens fall upon me,' he said to his father, the king, 'I must go out into the world, travel about, and find out all there is to know. Then I will return and take up my duties. Do I have your permission to go?'

"The king, who was a wise man, kissed his son on both cheeks and blessed him and sent him on his way. The prince wore simple country clothes that he had borrowed from one of the men on his estate, and he carried with him no more than a bundle of bread and cheese and, in his hand, a staff.

"With every league the prince put between himself and the palace, he felt the burdens of duty fall from him until, after two days on the road, he felt as light as a feather and as if he could walk forever . . ."

The story reached out to Colin as if it had been

written for him, as if Gwynne were the princess he must marry, as if sheep-herding were his princely duty. He settled himself more comfortably with his back against a warm rock and continued to read. The story twisted and turned, as the young prince's path turned and twisted. In a while his way became darker as he encountered sorrow, loss, pain, hunger, and even injustice. By the time he had finished his journey, he was bowed down by the weight of all the sorrows he had discovered as he crossed his father's kingdom. At the end of the story he reached home and gladly took up again the burdens and duties to which he had been born: his inheritance, his future wife, his life as servant to his people. "But I will never forget the burdens which others are forced to bear," he promised his old father. "And I will do what I may to lighten them."

An unexpected shiver ran down Colin's back. Surely the story had not so affected him? But when he looked up in surprise he saw that the sun had slipped behind a cloud and, in the west, across the wide expanse of ocean, an ominous black roll was approaching the island.

Shaking off the spell of the story, he packed the books back into their little chest, pushing down the hasps so that the watertight seal of leather inside the lid was snug. He locked it once more and slipped the leather thong with its key over his head. He was about to return the box to its hiding place when he stopped.

I should hide it in a place that only I know of, he thought craftily, and remembered a spot that had been a favourite when he was a child: a real cave, big enough to creep into, well above the highest tides. It was almost invisible from outside, looking like no more than a large crack in the rock. But once a person had squeezed through the narrow entrance passage, he would come upon a clean sandy cave. Colin had hidden in it often as a child and had never been discovered.

He found it now and wriggled through—it was a tighter fit than it had been five years ago—and remembered as he did so that above the entrance was a ridge of rock, a small natural shelf, just big enough to hold the box. Even if anyone—such as Jennifer— were to discover the cave, she would still be unlikely to find the box hidden so cleverly above the opening.

As Colin climbed the cliff path and jogged home- ward through the heather, he found himself puzzling at his motives. *Why did I save the books instead of leaving them on the beach for the tide to take?* The disappointment he had felt that the "treasure" Jennifer had spoken of was neither gold nor anything else of value was still bitter in his mouth. Yet he had gone out of his way to save the books, which were useless—if not actually evil.

Why? His actions made no sense. *And where has the time gone? The whole morning vanished in a flash, with no salvage wood nor any other excuse for my absence. Father will be angry and rightly so.* It was as if the story had held him spellbound. How was he to explain where he had been and what he had been doing?

But, as it happened, there was no need for excuses.

As he reached the outskirts of Merton Town, the roll of dark cloud he had seen in the distance was darkening the sky overhead and the wind was rising rapidly. There were the goats to herd safely into their shed, the outside ladder to the roof to secure, a dozen small jobs to be tackled before the storm. The chickens were shooed into their coop, not so difficult a chore since it was now so dark that many of them had already gone to roost as if it were nightfall. He helped Etta and Jennifer fill all their water pails, for who knew how long the storm might last?

By the time all this was done, the sound of the wind had risen to a shrill whine and the stones that weighed down the nets across the roofs of the houses—nets that held the thatch secure against such storms as this—were swaying to and fro at the ends of their ropes, cracking in a wild rhythm against the stone walls of the houses.

It was a rhythm that was as familiar in its way as was the sound of the lark on a fine summer's day. The harsh music warned him—and everyone else in Merton Town—of the severity of the approaching storm. The rattle of the stones was a steady *bonk-bonk-bonk* against the walls. The wind was from the northwest. Behind it, like dark fabric cut from the loom, the line of black cloud unrolled and covered the sky.

Colin pitied the sheep still out on the grazing grounds, but they must weather the storm on their own, as they were used to. They were a tough breed, these island sheep, and they knew enough to huddle close together for protection against the elements.

It wasn't until the last goat and chicken had been secured and all that could be had been tied down that they had time to take a breath and wipe the sweat from their faces. Colin glanced at Jennifer, wondering what the Stranger would make of an Ariban storm. She seemed calm and unafraid, lending a hand where she was able, keeping out of the way when she could not help.

Hedda secured the last shutter on the south-facing window. She stopped to count the ships in the harbour. "Three ships not back yet," she said grimly.

"Can you tell whose?" Fergus looked over her shoulder, his hand on the shutter.

She shook her head, finished closing and securing the shutter, and lit the oil lamp on the table. "Pray they return safely," she whispered as she stirred up the fire.

Colin stooped to place another block of peat on the hot ashes and, as he did so, the key swung forward from its hiding place inside his shirt. He heard Etta's indrawn breath as he felt it swing loose, and his hand was on it at once, tucking it safely out of sight. He knelt by the hearth, coaxing the fire into life with the bellows. Had Jennifer seen the key? He told himself that it didn't matter, that by rights of salvage the box and its contents were his. For what they were worth.

Now I must decide what to do with the books, how to turn them to my best advantage, he plotted. Once the storm was over, he should take them to Elder Shepherd and explain where he had found them. That was the safe and proper course. *Or I might offer them to Jennifer in exchange for her story about the world out there, beyond Ariban.* That was an exciting possibility. Or he could keep them secretly and continue to read them. The thought slid unbidden into his mind, and he felt an unfamiliar thrill at the power these choices gave him.

Once upon a time there was a prince whose future was bound by duty . . .

What was the point of the story? What did it mean—if anything? After all, he told himself, it wasn't true. It was lies, all lies. So why did his mind keep coming back to it?

Bound by duty. His life on Ariban was like that, wasn't it? Marrying Gwynne. Herding sheep. Raising children and teaching them to herd more sheep. A future bounded by the shores of the Isle of Ariban. Holding them in . . .

"But that is what we do," he argued with himself.

"What did you say, son?"

Startled, he looked up from the fire to meet his father's enquiring gaze. Had he spoken out loud? He shook his head. They were crazy thoughts anyway, best forgotten. He wondered if Jennifer was some kind of witch and if the books contained evil spells. Certainly he had never had ideas like this before she had come to Ariban.

The wind slammed against the house so hard that the shutters shook and the ballast stones swayed and clunked against the walls. Fergus whittled at a piece of wood, turning it into a spoon. Hedda gave Etta a handful of raw wool to clean and pulled her spinning wheel towards her. The passage of a storm, however severe, was no excuse for idleness. Only Jennifer sat motionless, her hands in her lap. Colin saw her lips move and wondered, fancifully, if she were weaving another story from the warp and weft of the storm itself.

She must have felt his eyes on her, for she looked up suddenly, her blue eyes flashing in the flicker of the oil lamp. Was she angry with him? Automatically his hand went to his shirt to make sure the key was securely hidden. Her eyes followed the movement of his hand, and he knew that she guessed what he had done. He saw her small hands double into fists.

"That fire will do fine by itself now, Colin," his mother told him. "Put the pot on to boil. Then you and Jennifer can chop vegetables for supper."

As they stood at the table he whispered to her, "There is a law of salvage on Ariban. He who first claims the wreckage from a storm has the rights to it for eight days."

"I know that," she said, furiously slicing an onion. "Etta told me. But—"

"But what?" he said rudely.

"The key is mine," she whispered so that the others would not hear. "You stole it."

He shrugged and gave a forced laugh. "It is only borrowed."

"Then give it back," she hissed.

"Perhaps I've not finished with it yet."

She gave him a small smile with no humour in it. "So you have discovered my treasure and you know it to be neither gold nor precious stones. So why—?"

"You deceived me." He thumped his knife through a particularly tough turnip. "You said it was even richer."

71

"And so it is," she said tranquilly.

"Books filled with stories," he snapped. "Lies, all of them. I could tell the Elders what you are."

"So you could. But I have already told them I was a storyteller."

"Yes, but you made it sound like something else. Something innocent, like history."

"And so it is. Stories connect past and present. They are a guide left by the wise old ones for our future help."

"Stories of dragons and princesses? Of princes seeking their fortune?" he mocked. "What is real about these?"

"They are stories of young women learning to face their innermost fears instead of running away from them. Of young men making choices founded on truths they have discovered for themselves, not upon habit or hearsay—"

"How you two chatter," Hedda interrupted. "The water is boiling. Aren't those vegetables ready yet?"

"Just done." Colin scooped the chopped turnips, carrots, potatoes, and onions into the water bubbling on the stove. He didn't understand a word that Jennifer had said, but he felt uneasily that he had somehow come off the worse in their argument.

CHAPTER FOUR

T he wind blew and shook the door and shutters as Hedda spooned soup into bowls and Etta put the bread board on the table. Fergus automatically gave thanks and they ate in silence, with a background of rocks thunking against the house, of wind moaning and ropes thrumming. When the noise suddenly ceased, they all looked up in shock. There was an ominous silence, then it began again with a different voice.

"It's shifted to the southeast," Fergus said grimly. "It'll be blowing towards the harbour."

"If there are still ships out there, Heaven pity them!" Hedda exclaimed. "Men may well be lost tonight."

There was no need for further talk. They pushed back their chairs and snatched up cloaks, wrapping them tightly around them. Jennifer looked in bewilderment from one to another.

"You can stay here," Colin said gruffly. "You don't have to come."

But Etta found a heavy cloak for Jennifer and, when Fergus pulled open the door, they all plunged out into the tearing, blustering windswept world. Slipping and sliding on the wet cobbles, they struggled in the teeth of the wind down towards Merton Harbour.

As they staggered down the road to the harbour wall, Etta breathlessly explained the danger to Jennifer. "The wind's from the southeast. That almost *never* happens. Merton Harbour is the safest in the world, but to come into it with a southeast wind at your back, that's death, they say. Mother counted three ships missing when the storm began. Who knows if they've got safely to their berths."

Since Fergus was a shepherd rather than a fisherman, their cottage was on the northern outskirts of Merton, closer to the grazing grounds than to the sea, so by the time they reached the harbour wall it was already crowded. More than a hundred men and women stood in silence, while the small children huddled close to their mothers' skirts. Every eye was on the narrow entrance to the harbour and on the two fishing boats struggling to gain the safety of its protecting walls.

"Why don't they just stand out to sea till the wind dies down?" Jennifer asked.

Before Etta could answer, a woman standing nearby with her arms folded across her chest, hugging her cloak to her, turned and spoke angrily.

"Can you not see how the wind drives them

towards the rocks, Stranger? They are trapped. There is only one safe place now and that is within the harbour. All else is death."

"You would think any fool would know that," another woman added. "In all my thirty-two years on Ariban, I can remember the wind blowing from that quarter only once. It is a curse on us all." She turned and spat on the cobbles at Jennifer's feet. Colin stepped forward angrily, but Hedda's hand was on his arm, pulling him back.

A sudden murmur swept across the crowd. Fingers pointed. "Look there," someone shouted, and the people turned their angry gazes from Jennifer to stare out into the storm.

The first fishing boat, its sail taut with the wind, was heading full tilt towards the rocks that guarded the narrow entrance. Just as it seemed to everyone that the small boat would sail right onto the rocks, they saw the sail drop. It had been perfectly judged. The small craft skimmed past the rocks, through the gap in the harbour wall, and safely into the calmer water within.

A ragged cheer went up from the crowd.

"'Tis Kevin's boat."

"Aye, there's a sailor with skill!"

"What a risk, though!"

"Reckon it paid off. He won through. Who's still out there?"

"Irving and Duff."

"I see only the one boat."

"The other's still offshore behind the north headland."

Colin wriggled from his mother's grasp and made his way along the south side of the harbour wall, where only a few men stood hunched against the wind. If the two remaining boats were approaching the harbour from the northeast, they would be more likely to run afoul of the rocks to the south of the harbour as they swung around for a clear approach.

Once away from the protection of the crowd, Colin staggered as the full force of the wind hit him. The cobbles were slippery with rain. Close to the headland, the wild waves dashed themselves to pieces on the rocks and were flung into the faces of the watchers in a rain of spume. He licked the caked salt from his lips and wondered what it would be like to be one of these sailors, fighting for his life, on a knife's edge between safety and drowning. More exciting by far than being a mere shepherd. The stuff of story.

Once upon a time there was a young fisherman . . . The words drifted, ready-made, into his mind. He pushed away the alien thought. This was not the way of the people of Ariban. Good events and bad alike were shrugged off, not spoken of, but buried and forgotten. Or *were* they entirely forgotten? There were widows in this silent crowd remembering the day when their man had not come home, the day when they knew that their children would be raised fatherless.

Looking back into the comparative quiet of the harbour, Colin could see Kevin's boat—its heavy sail lying in a soggy pile on the deck—making its way slowly towards its moorings. The two men laboured with the oars to regain some of the speed they had lost when they dropped their sail.

Once Colin had reached the end of the breakwater, he could see the second boat clearly through the blowing spume. Its skipper was obviously planning the same manoeuvre that Kevin had so successfully completed. Under full sail the small craft was approaching the shore with the force of the gale behind it. Unlike the first boat, though, this one had not swung as far south, Colin reckoned. If they were to drop the sail now, as Kevin had done, the wind would sweep them past the safety of the opening and batter them to pieces on the rocks outside the harbour.

This was Irving's boat. As it drew closer to the rocks, Colin could see clearly the ruddy hair of its skipper, darkened by rain and sea. The danger was obviously as clear to him as it was to those ashore; he was keeping his sail full, but turning his boat so that the wind caught the sail on his port quarter. The boat skidded sideways towards the opening.

It was a desperate move. Any sudden gust or change in wind direction would send them heeling over, swamped and out of control. There was silence on shore. It was so quiet that, even over the screaming wind, those close to the entrance of the harbour could hear the hoarse shouts of the skipper to his mate.

In the single heartbeat between safety and disaster, when it seemed that his boat must be crushed against the harbour wall, Irving dropped his sail. Colin caught his breath. *He's mad*, he thought. But the small craft righted itself and slid safely into the harbour, grazing the rocks at the end of the breakwater with a scrunch of splitting timbers. Cheers rose above the roar of the waves. From the harbour wall they could not yet see what was clear to Colin, perched on the rocks at the harbour entrance: the boat's side was stove in.

Like a beached whale, Irving's boat wallowed slowly in the deep and swirling waters. In a short time it would be submerged. He could see Irving and his crew pull out the oars, desperately digging them into the tumultuous sea. There was only one way.

"A rope!" Colin yelled, and an end was thrown down to him. Without giving himself time to think, he twisted it around his hand and flung himself into the water. The coldness was like a vice tightening around his chest, freezing his legs. He threw back his head from the waves and gasped. Then he began to struggle towards the sinking boat. With each painful length he gained, the wet rope seemed heavier. He could feel it pulling him down. He sank beneath the waves and came up, coughing and spitting, gasping for air. *I can't*, he thought. *Easier just to shut my eyes and sink . . .*

Once upon a time there was a young prince . . . He struggled on. Now he was close enough to the fishing boat to read the name on her side—*Seagull*—almost at water level. He could feel himself sinking again and flailed out desperately. One hand was caught in a firm grasp. The rope was prised from his other hand; he'd held it so tightly that now he could hardly let go. Then strong arms were under his armpits, and he was being hauled up and rolled over the thwart. He was kneeling on the bottom boards amid the swirling water, coughing and gasping.

When he had recovered, he saw that Irving and his mate had hitched the end of rope to the iron ring in the boat's bow. Many willing hands hauled the water-logged and battered boat towards the shore. Painfully, handspan by handspan, they were pulled to safety, the water swirling level with the gunwales. He could hardly hear its keel grating on the pebbles for the sound of cheering from the crowd.

Then he was being helped ashore and his dripping body wrapped in a blanket against the cruel wind. Hands patted his back. *Like a prince*, he thought. He felt wonderful, important, the fear and the pain in his chest gone. *I will never forget this day*, he thought, and regretted that the people of Ariban did not cele-brate such events in story or song. *Why, I could have been famous!*

Just as this absurd thought flashed through his head, the hands that had been patting him dropped away. People turned from him to stare eastward into the storm.

"Here comes *Marlin*!"

Duff's ship was careering directly towards the opening in a flurry of white water. There was a clam-our of voices.

"She's coming in under full sail!" someone gasped.

"Duff saw the way the wind was changing, what happened to Irving!" cried another.

"She'll make it. Oh, Duff, my man, what a sailor you are!" Colin turned at the woman's voice and recognized her as Duff's wife—and the woman who had spat at Jennifer. Her cloak had fallen open and the wind-blown spray soaked her woollen blouse and skirt unnoticed. She stood with her hands clasped to her mouth. "Come on, dear one. Come on," she urged.

For ten heartbeats or so, it seemed to those ashore that *Marlin* would reach safe harbour. Then there came a crack, as sudden as a thunder clap. A groan went up from the crowd and, in the time between one heartbeat and the next, the mast snapped like a twig; the sail, already heavy with rain and spray, fell into the water.

Before the horrified eyes of the people of Merton Town, the sail was pulled beneath the water, dragging *Marlin* and her crew with it. Less than a rope's throw from safety, the boat disappeared beneath the waves that battered the north headland.

The wail from Duff's widow was like a knife slicing through the silence. "My husband. My son!" The fisher wives closed around her, hands patting her shoulders, stroking her arms, offering their wordless sympathy.

"They should let her weep, not stifle her grief," Colin heard Jennifer murmur. *That is not our way*, he was about to retort, but then he was surrounded by fisherfolk, with Irving and his wife, the crew and their families, all wanting to shake his hand, to pat his shoulder. It was almost as if the death of Duff that they had just witnessed made it clearer just how close the others had come to losing *their* lives as well.

He felt borne up by the warmth of their praise, no longer aware of the cold of his soaking shirt and breeches. Then Elder Fisher strode through the crowd. Even wrapped in his cloak, as they all were, without his necklace and the formal gaff of his office, he was an imposing figure. Silently the crowd drew back to give him room.

He stopped in front of Colin, and Colin glowed at the approval in the old man's piercing eyes. "You have done well, Colin, son of Fergus, and your bravery will not be forgotten." He nodded and passed on through the crowd to where Duff's widow, Nola, stood silently, surrounded by her comforters.

"Elder Fisher," she cried out as soon as she saw him. "What will become of me now? Of me and my fatherless children?"

"It is just a formal appeal," Colin whispered to Jennifer. "She knows she will never be neglected, not here on Ariban."

The reply of Elder Fisher was also formal. "Nola, wife of Duff, we hear you. You and your children will never want for fish and meat, for milk and bread. Your peat will be cut and your roof repaired. You have the word of the people of Merton Town."

A murmur of agreement ran through the crowd at the Elder's pledge. Then Gwynne appeared, wedging herself between him and Jennifer, and slipped her hand into his. "What a great thing you did today, Colin. I am proud of you."

He looked down at her and then across at the tall figure of Jennifer, standing silently just beyond her, wrapped in the borrowed cloak, her face almost hidden in its hood.

I have Gwynne's approval. And her grandfather's. So why do I look for something from Jennifer? Does she think I am a hero also, someone worthy of one of her stories? And if so, why does she not tell me? He began to shiver violently as the cold penetrated the blanket that had been wrapped around him. *I'm a fool*, he told himself. *Why do I need a Stranger's approval, when I have that of the people of Ariban?*

"Come, we must get you home and into warm clothes," said Gwynne practically. "I will walk with you up the hill."

She chatted lightly as they walked. He was never able to remember anything she said. His mind roiled like the storm clouds still scudding overhead. *What do I want? To be a shepherd like my father? To marry Gwynne and raise a family here on Ariban where I belong? To live and die here? And why not? Ariban is beautiful. Life here is good. I can be happy.*

Can't I?

Gwynne left him at his door, and his mother, having shooed Etta and Jennifer up to the attic, heated water, stripped off his clothes, and set him in a bath in front of a good fire. It wasn't until he was once again warmly dressed and they were all seated around the table to finish their interrupted meal that his mother flung a question at him like a stone.

"*Why*, son? Why did you risk your life? You are not even a fisher."

He hesitated, spoon between bowl and mouth.

Why indeed? *To be a hero* was not an answer that would make any sense on practical Ariban.

Why had he done it? Had there been any deliberate thought between the knowledge that Irving's boat was foundering and his plunge into the raging waters? *I could have died*, he thought in sudden shock, and put his spoon down.

"You could have died!" His mother echoed his thought. "We could have lost our only son."

He shook his head. He was suddenly enormously tired, stupid with sleep. "I don't know, Mother. I just did."

He stared into his wooden soup bowl, feeling, rather than seeing, Jennifer's blue eyes upon him. *Does she understand why I did it? Can she make sense of the turmoil inside my head?*

He blundered to his feet. "I'm off to bed. Good night, Mother. Good night, Father. Good night all," he added in a general way, not naming Etta or Jennifer.

"You did well, son," Fergus said gruffly. "I'm proud of you."

With these words—from a man of very few words—like a warm blanket around him, Colin stumbled up the ladder to the attic, unlaced his shoes, fell onto his bed, and was instantly asleep.

Colin slept late the next day, waking to one of Ariban's perfect mornings. It was as if the angry storm had washed the island clean, so that it sparkled under a sky of intense blueness. *Almost as blue as her eyes*, he found himself thinking as he pushed the shutter open and looked past the outskirts of Merton Town to the fresh green of the grazing grounds.

He straightened his sleep-rumpled clothes, laced on his shoes, and climbed down into the kitchen. *She* wasn't there, nor was Etta.

"Your breakfast is on the hob," his mother said, not pausing in her spinning.

He spooned the gruel into a bowl. "Where are the girls?" He tried to keep his voice casual.

She looked at him sharply, without changing the rhythm of her spinning. "I sent them down to the shop to get more purple-root to dye the wool. They should be back by now."

He scooped up the gruel, scraped the bowl clean, and set it with the others to be washed. "Your father'll want you to help repair the storm damage, but first go down and hurry the girls back. I need that purple-root. Today's a great day for dyeing and drying."

Willingly Colin left the house and walked briskly down to the shop of the town herbalist. Her skill at picking and preparing leaves and roots was in large part responsible for the fame of Ariban's wools, the colours foreigners loved.

As he approached the crossroads, he could hear raised voices and see that a crowd was beginning to gather. Forgetting his errand, he ran to join it. As he was recognized, the crowd parted and he found himself at the centre of the dispute, facing the widow Nola.

The widow's hair was unkempt, her eyes wild, and spittle flew from her lips as she pointed a shaking finger at Etta and Jennifer, trapped within the packed crowd.

"Never before has there been a disaster such as this. Aye, our men have died at sea, but never so close to the safety of the harbour." She raised her right arm and pointed a shaking finger at Jennifer, who stood, proud and unmoving, her arm around Etta.

"It is you who have brought calamity to Ariban. You, Stranger. You are a curse to us all. There is no luck in you. Woe to you and to those who have sheltered you." Her mad eyes now turned to Colin, and her wavering finger pointed at him. "It is *you* who snatched her from the sea. *You* who cheated the sea of its rightful prize. Now the sea has taken my husband and son instead of this wicked woman."

Her hands went to cover her face. "Oh, what will become of me and mine?"

"Elder Fisher has pledged . . ." Colin ventured, but then his eyes dropped before the hatred in hers.

"Can he bring back the love of my man? Can he bring back those strong arms around me?" Her voice rose to a scream. A murmur of sympathy spread through the crowd, a murmur that rose to anger.

"Peace, woman!" At the sound of Elder Fisher's voice there was silence. The crowd parted to allow him to stride to the centre—to stand between the widow on one side, and Colin, Etta, and Jennifer on the other.

Colin drew a breath of relief. He had never witnessed the anger of a crowd before. It was more terrifying than the storm waves had been, and he had

85

been wondering how he could snatch the girls away and spirit them safely home.

"Peace," the Elder said again, his arms raised. "You know we have pledged you support, widow Nola. What else do you ask?"

"It is not enough, Elder Fisher. My husband and my eldest son—both gone. I ask repayment for their loss."

"What repayment?"

"A life for a life, Elder Fisher. *Hers*." She pointed at Jennifer. "And *his* for bringing this curse upon us. She should have died on the shore where she was found. She was the sea's and the sea was cheated." And now her accusing finger pointed straight at Colin. "Two lives for two lives, Elder Fisher."

Colin felt as if her finger were spearing him through the heart. He couldn't breathe. The sweat trickled in cold drops down his forehead. A long way off he heard the murmur of the crowd. Different voices. Arguing for and against.

"Yes, it is his fault as much as hers. He is as guilty."

"But it was he who risked his life to rescue Irving and his son and bring *Seagull* safe ashore," another voice protested.

"The family of Fergus has always been respected."

"Nevertheless they brought the woman here."

The argument went on, tossed to and fro like a ball.

It was interrupted by a child's shrill voice. "Etta tells stories." It broke through the murmurs and arguments. Every head turned. It was Gwynne's younger sister who had spoken.

Elder Fisher beckoned to her and, with her elder sister Gwynne's arm around her shoulder, she came and stood directly in front of him. "That is a grave accusation, Colleen. Are you sure you know what you are saying?"

Gwynne spoke for her sister. "Etta told the young ones a wicked story about princesses and dragons."

"Let the child speak for herself, Granddaughter," the Elder reproved.

"It was at the Sunday picnic. It was a nice story, Grandfather. It told us not to be afraid, but to stand up to our fear."

"But it was a lie, Grandfather," Gwynne interrupted again. "The Stranger told Etta the story, and the Stranger is a liar."

Her voice was bitter with spite. Surely that must be evident to everyone here, thought Colin. He opened his mouth to protest that it was Gwynne's envy of Jennifer that was the reason for her accusation, but then he closed it again. Whatever he said would only incriminate himself and his family further. But why now? She had seemed all favour and sweetness when she had walked home with him last night.

He tried to remember what they had talked about, but all that came back to him were her words, going on and on. And his silence.

What have I done?

Elder Fisher stood tall, his arms above his head. "Hear this, people of Merton. At the full moon we will hold a Moot. Every man and woman of Merton Town will be entitled to speak for or against the widow Nola's claim of a life for a life: the stranger

Jennifer's for Duff, and that of Colin, son of Fergus and Hedda, for Duff's son. Elder Shepherd and I will sit in judgement at the Moot."

There was a murmur of approval.

Elder Fisher raised his voice. "Until that time the Stranger will continue to lodge in the house of Fergus and Hedda. She will not speak to anyone outside that family. Colin, son of Fergus, you will take my words to your parents. Tell them this: guard your children closely and do not allow *them* to pass on any lies or deceits that the Stranger may speak. If you fail to obey my orders, you will be considered as guilty as the Stranger and Colin, and you also will be tried under the law of the Moot." The Elder turned and strode through the silent crowd, which closed behind him.

Colin felt the people surrounding him draw back as if he were infected with some plague—these same people who, only the night before, had praised him for his bravery. He gritted his teeth, held his head high, and tried to keep his voice steady. "Come, Etta. Mother wants you and Jennifer back home."

He pushed them ahead of him and, as the crowd separated to let them pass, he turned to look at Gwynne. *Your doing*, he silently accused her. *You have betrayed me and my family.* He knew that Colleen was a shy child, not unlike Etta, and he was certain that she would never have spoken up unless she had been forced into it by her strong-willed elder sister.

Gwynne's eyes slid away from his, and he turned and followed the girls up the hill. *To think we were to be married at Midsummer*, he thought. It won't happen now, not after Colleen's accusation. Elder Fisher will never permit it. He told himself that he had had a lucky escape, that to be married to a spiteful woman would not make for a happy life.

Lucky? a cynical voice inside him retorted. *If they decide to exile or execute you, it will not be much of an escape.* For the first time, the actual words of Elder Fisher sank into his consciousness. *A life for a life.*

Back at the house Colin delivered the Elder's message, word for word. His mother let out a great scream, such as he had never heard before, while his father turned white and left the house. Then his mother grimly put the purple-root to boil and set Jennifer and Etta to washing the skeins of wool she had been spinning all spring.

"I'm sorry, Mother," he pleaded.

"Go help your father," was all she said. The rest of the day was spent in silence, except for necessary commands, such as "hold that rail steady" and "fetch my hammer".

As he worked he could see Jennifer briskly soaking wool in barrels of rainwater and handing them to Hedda to immerse in the simmering dye. *Does she not understand that she may be sentenced to death? That I, too . . . ?* Waves of panic overcame him, in which he was deaf to his father's orders, but stood numbly shivering until they subsided.

A day's silent work ended in silent supper and bed. Sleep did not come easily. He could hear Jennifer murmuring to Etta, but had no inclination to eavesdrop upon her lies. *It is all her fault*, he thought angrily. When the panic returned he told himself, *They won't hurt us. Not on Ariban.* But then the half-forgotten story of Alan came into his mind and haunted his sleepless night.

The following morning, as they sat around the breakfast table, he blurted his question into the silence.

"Whatever became of Alan?"

Etta stared. "What do you mean, Colin? There's no one called Alan on Ariban."

"I know that. But there was once. I don't remember much about him. It was many years ago, before you were born, I reckon. All I remember is that he did something bad—told stories or dreamed dreams. He was condemned to death. And that is all I know. His name is not spoken, and no one since has ever given the name 'Alan' to a child. What really happened to him, Father?"

"Why must you bring this up now, of all times?" Hedda put her spoon down, and Colin saw tears come to her eyes.

"As you said, it is not to be spoken of," Fergus added firmly.

"Maybe it should be," Colin argued. "Our whole family is accused of harbouring a witch. It is supposed to be all my fault for bringing her to Merton instead of allowing her to die on the beach. It is serious enough for a Moot to be called. I need to know what these accusations mean. What will become of us?"

Hedda stared at Fergus in the thickening silence. Then she spoke reluctantly. "Tell them, husband."

Fergus sighed heavily. Colin could feel the pain filling the small room like a fog. "It is a fair question and it deserves an answer. You are right. Alan was a dreamer. He was accused and found guilty under the age-old laws of Ariban."

"What happened to him?"

"He jumped into the sea at South Peak and was dashed to his death on the rocks below. His body was washed out to sea."

Colin shivered as if it were his body plunging from the cliff top into the relentless sea. "Was he—?" Colin stopped and began again. "Did he jump of his own free will?"

"The assembly of all the people of Ariban, Merton Town and Lynn-by-the-Lake, decided in Moot assembly that he was guilty. His lies and stories were a danger to the young people of Ariban, especially to the sons of fishers, drawing them away from their allotted life . . ."

"So he didn't die willingly?"

Fergus shook his head. "He was driven up the hill to the top of the Peak. It was the decision of all the people of Ariban. We were all party to it."

"How old was this Alan, Father?"

"Younger than you, Colin. He was the son of a fisherman from Lynn-by-the-Lake."

Jennifer gasped. "A *youth*? You murdered one of your own children? In heaven's name, why?"

"His ideas were dangerous. They could have destroyed the whole community."

"The ideas of one *child*?"

"You are a stranger. You do not know our ways." Hedda twisted her hands together as she spoke. "When we gather blaeberries for the winter, we pick through them very carefully, especially if there has been much rain. It takes only one mouldy berry to spoil the whole pailful. So it must be found and thrown out."

"But a human being is not a berry! A boy, like this poor Alan, is the sum of his memories, his learning, and—yes—his *dreams*. His past as well as his present and future. The future of a child is not like the unchanging future of a berry—either to be eaten now or to be dried and eaten later in the winter months. The future of a child is more like the growth of a tree. There is the healthy root stock, which is the past, the parenting, the memories; then there is the trunk, growing sturdier year by year, which is the present; then there are the branches, dividing into smaller branches and into twigs and twiglets—all the possible futures between which the growing child must choose wisely, choose through dreaming and imagining . . ."

"But there are no trees on Ariban," Etta interrupted.

"Nor any dreaming or imagining!" Jennifer exclaimed in despair. "So to your shame, you cut down the sapling that would have become the adult 'Alan'. And now you will never know what he might have been. He is not spoken of. He is not remembered, except in the passing down of the lore that 'Alan' is not a lucky name to give a child."

Etta's eyes had been fixed on Jennifer's as she

spoke. Now she said, "Someone must remember. Didn't Alan have a mother and father?"

The innocent question fell into a silence that grew more uneasy with each breath. Colin saw Hedda and Fergus exchange glances, but they said nothing.

"You didn't kill them *too*, did you?" Jennifer exclaimed in horror.

Fergus flushed. "We are good law-abiding people on Ariban. Not murderers. The mother was a widow named Aileen. She was forgiven for not reporting her son's misdeeds to the Elders because of her husband's death at sea. It was felt that if the father had been alive, he would have whipped some sense into the boy."

"Is she still alive—Alan's mother?" Etta asked. "I've never heard the name Aileen."

"She lives—or did live—by herself in a cottage outside Lynn-by-the-Lake. And that is enough on this subject." Fergus pushed his chair roughly back from the table. "As for all this talk of trees, of imagining and dreaming, I charge you, children, not another word, or you'll have us all driven over the cliff. If I must whip you into silence, I will do it. Aye, even you, Colin, grown though you are. If I must starve you into obedience, I will do that too. And if, in spite of all, you disobey me, I will hand you over to Elder Shepherd. I have my wife, your mother, to protect. And protect her I will. Now I must go and see how well our sheep have weathered the storm."

He stood, shrugged on his sheepskin jacket, and pushed his feet into his shoes. "Father, may not I come too?" Colin asked, eager to be out of the house.

"No, you may not. For now you will stay close to home under your mother's eye." He left the house, slamming the door behind him.

Hedda ran her hands over her face, straightened her shoulders, and said briskly, "No reason to sit here mumchance. There is plenty of work for us all to do. Colin, you will go up on the roof and see if the thatch needs repairing after the storm. When you have done that, you can bring in more peat from the shed."

She got heavily to her feet, leaning on the table. Etta said timidly, "What about Jennifer and me?"

Hedda turned on her, hands on hips. "You will stay out of mischief. Go draw water and set it to boil. I have more wool to dye. Then you can chop the vegetables. And remember, not a word to anyone, not so much as a 'goodmorrow' if you meet people on the street or at the well. I want no gossip. No talk of the 'future'. Remember this, our future on Ariban is as secure as our past. We are born to be fishers or shepherds, and the wives of fishers or shepherds. That is the beginning and the end of it. So no more foolishness. You heard what your father said. You had best obey him. Believe me, he is a man of his word."

She settled herself at the loom and began to weave, throwing the shuttle with a quick flick of her wrist, pulling the beater towards her, feet on the treadles and hands on beater and shuttle in a harsh rhythm that shut out all possibility of discussion.

Wordlessly, Jennifer took up the pails and drew Etta out of the anger-filled house.

CHAPTER FIVE

From his position straddling the ridge of the roof, Colin saw Etta and Jennifer scurry down the cobbled street towards the town well—at least Etta was scurrying, looking fearfully from side to side. Jennifer walked tall, her movements graceful and dignified. Some of the smaller children were playing in the town square, but as the two girls approached, doors were opened, mothers called out, and the children were whisked quickly inside their homes. By the time the girls had reached the well and were beginning to fill their pails, the square was deserted.

Will it always be like this? Colin wondered. *Will our family never be forgiven for bringing the Stranger among us?*

A spark of anger began to grow inside him, small at first, like the embers of a fire first thing in the morning, hidden under its covering of peat, but growing, like the fire blown into life by the bellows, until it flamed through his whole body.

It's not fair. When I rescued Irving, I was treated like a hero by everyone in Merton Town. Now, two days later, everyone behaves as if our family has the plague. It's not my fault that I found her on the beach. It was just bad luck that it was I who discovered her. It could have been anyone.

It was her fault, really. The girl with the foreign-sounding name and the gaudy foreign clothes. The girl with the strange blue eyes. Her and her stories.

But I did hide the box. Why did I do that? I should have taken it straight to the Elders. If I had been honest and done that, our family would not be blamed for her lies and stories. Only she would.

He hadn't wanted her to go back to the cove and take the box, he told himself. He hadn't wanted *her* to have her stories, which must be the source of her power. That was his real reason for hiding the box, wasn't it?

Then why did I not take it straight to the Elders? I should have done that.

There seemed to be no answer to this. Colin sighed and tucked a loose bundle of reeds safely under the netting that covered the upper part of the roof. He began to check the ropes that hung from the netting, weighted by rocks that held down the thatch in times of storm. The two girls were returning from the well now, Etta struggling to carry a pail in both hands, while Jennifer trudged along with a yoke across her shoulders and a big pail hanging from each end. When the old yoke had broken, Colin remembered, he had carved the new one himself from a cast-up piece of mast.

I'm a good son. I do my duty. I don't deserve to be blamed for this, he told himself.

Jennifer tripped over a cobblestone and stopped to catch her breath and steady the pails. For an instant he felt sorry for her. Ariban must be very different from the world of castles and storytelling. She was trapped here against her will, her fate to be decided at the Moot.

But I am trapped too. I, too, have to face the Moot.

What can I do to prove my loyalty to the Elders? The question slid slyly into his mind, and, quick as a flash, the answer came.

I must take the box to Elder Shepherd at once, and then the blame will fall only on Jennifer and I will be free of it. And so will Etta and our parents, of course, he added hastily to himself.

He scrambled down the ladder that stood propped against the roof and landed on the ground just as the two girls approached the door. Etta smiled at him, obviously thankful to be safe home again, but there was no smile on Jennifer's face as she turned her dark blue eyes towards him. Sharp eyes that seemed to run through him, almost as if she were reading his thoughts. *Witch*, he told himself, and turned away uneasily, pretending to check the ends of the ropes fastened around the ballast stones.

It's not just for myself, he argued. *It's her or us. It's for Etta and Mother and Father too.*

Then why am I not going now, quickly, to get the box and give it to the Elder? He pushed the niggling thought away and went into the shed built onto the eastern side of the house. As he began to stack cakes of dried peat onto the small skid that stood there, he argued with himself.

There's no hurry. I needn't do anything right away. I can wait until it's needful. The Moot is not until next Sunday.

He hauled the skid to the door, pulled the string that lifted the door latch, and dragged it over to the fireplace. His mother didn't turn. *Slam* went the beater of the loom, *clack* went the treadles.

That'll be a length of extra-firm cloth, with all of Mother's anger behind it, he thought. He wondered if she were more angry at Jennifer for getting them into trouble, or with him for finding her. A strange thought flashed, unbidden, into his head. *Maybe she's angry for the boy, Alan, and his widowed mother.* He stacked the last peat in place and straightened up. *What had the women of Ariban thought back then, when Alan was driven to his death?*

"What are you staring at?" Hedda snapped. "Have you no work to do?"

"I've mended the roof as you asked, Mother, and brought in the peat." He kept his voice soft, reasonable-sounding, but it didn't seem to help.

"Hmm." She seemed to be searching for something impudent in his manner. She failed to find it and returned to the rhythm of the shuttle, beater, and treadles. At the table, the girls were chopping the eternal-seeming vegetables. *At least I'm not a girl,* he thought.

"Go find your father, then," Hedda snapped over

her shoulder. "He's bound to have something for you to do that'll keep you out of mischief."

But Father doesn't want to see me, Colin thought, hesitating. *And neither does Mother. Why? I've done nothing wrong. Not really.* He clenched his teeth, shrugged into his sheepskin jerkin, and stamped out of the house.

He came upon his father at the north end of the grazing grounds. Fergus had checked on all his sheep after the storm and found one missing. "Patch. She's always been a wanderer and now she's surpassed herself. I've searched as far as the south side of Lynn Lake, so she's probably gone north of the lake."

"Don't worry, Father. I'll find her," said Colin eagerly. He knew that the cross old ewe, with the brown spot like a dab of paint on her left ear, was a favourite of his father's. If he could find her and return her safely to the herd, perhaps his father would forgive him for bringing the Stranger and all her trouble to their house.

He headed northeast across the meadowland towards Lynn Lake, glad to be alone with his thoughts, free of his mother's anger and the feeling of oppression that hung over what had, until now, always seemed a peaceable house. As he walked he tried to make up his mind about what he had to do. But other thoughts kept floating up and getting in the way of any decision.

There was the fact that her eyes were so large and of such a brilliant, almost unnatural, blue. Most islanders had eyes that were grey or pale blue. Gwynne's were noticeably small, as if she were always squinting at the sun. Her skin was freckled too, whereas Jennifer's was as white as a young child's. He wondered if she had ever worked under the sun, picking berries, milking goats, or cutting peat, before she came to Ariban. Had her life always been lived in castles and great houses among noble men and women? Her voice, too, was quiet and melodious. Gwynne's was sometimes shrill, especially if her will was crossed.

Colin sighed and walked more and more quickly, as if by so doing he could escape his troublesome thoughts. He had known since he was twelve years old that he was to marry Gwynne. That was how such matters were always arranged on Ariban; the parents knew best who was suited to whom, and a sober arrangement of this kind avoided ill feelings and other such problems.

Until last week he had not thought much about the arrangement one way or the other. But recently he found himself wondering what his life would be like, sitting opposite Gwynne at their own table, hearing her voice day in, day out.

"That is the way life is," he told himself firmly, remembering his mother's words. *We do not need dreams or talk about the future here on Ariban. We are born to be fishermen or shepherds or the wives of fishermen and shepherds. That is the beginning and the end of it.*

Unbidden, the words of the story he had read in Half-Moon Cove came back to him. *Once upon a time there was a prince whose future was bound by duty . . .*

The prince had escaped for a time, Colin remembered, to have great adventures in many places. Certainly he had returned to take up his duties in the end, but the point of the story was, Colin now realized for the first time, that he returned of his own free will with the knowledge he had acquired in the great world outside his own small kingdom. And he was the better for it. As were his subjects. Yes, that was what the story was really about.

But he was no prince, he reminded himself grimly. Next Sunday he must face the judgement of the Moot. Even if all went well, Elder Fisher might hesitate to give his granddaughter in marriage to a troublemaker.

By now Colin had reached the west end of Lynn Lake. It was shallow and muddy, edged with the rushes that were cut every autumn to mend the thatches of the houses in Merton and Lynn-by-the-Lake. As he walked slowly around its edge, taking care to avoid the boggy areas, he called half-heartedly, "Patch, Patch! Where are you, stupid sheep?"

She was a good ewe, even though her wandering habits were a nuisance, and she produced a healthy lamb or two each spring, as well as a goodly quantity of fine wool.

He had reached the northern side of the lake and was turning eastward towards the village of Lynn when he heard a faint bleat in answer to his call. He climbed to an outcrop of rock among the coarse marsh grass to get a better view. He called again, and an answering bleat came from over to the east. He shaded his eyes and peered in that direction, but could see nothing. There was no discernible movement, and no errant ewe came trotting towards him. Just a duck flapping out of the water and the cry of a distant curlew.

She's bogged down, silly creature, he thought grimly, and set off eastward, hoping he would reach her before she sank under the mud and was lost.

The edge of the lake was rimmed with patches of bright green sphagnum moss—a clear warning to stay away, for under the network of moss was nothing more solid than a gruel-like mud, dangerous to man and beast alike. Colin walked slowly, testing every step, stopping now and then to scan the surrounding ground.

He found a muddy scar in the moss. Almost immediately he saw the place where pieces of turf and moss had been torn by the scrabbling of frantic hooves. And there she was, the foolish ewe, muddied from head to tail, so it was no wonder that he had not been able to see her sooner. She had managed to heave her body onto a tussock of somewhat firmer grass, and there she hung, unable to move forward or back.

She was a rope's throw from solid shore. Even if he could reach her, he would never be able to drag her back and would probably drown in the mud himself. He was standing, wondering what to do, when she caught sight of him. Her eyes rolled back in her head so he could see the whites, and she gave a despairing bleat.

The pathetic sound stirred Colin into action. He couldn't save the ewe by himself, but perhaps with the help of a nearby shepherd . . . He looked around. The village of Lynn-by-the-Lake was out of sight over a low rise, but he could see the thatched roof of a small cottage in a fold of land about halfway between him and the village. He began to run, leaping tussocks of heather, skirting thickets of bramble and briar.

If no one's home I can borrow a ladder and a rope, though it'll be harder to manage by myself, he thought breathlessly as he ran.

His fist thudded on the door. There was no response.

"Help!" he yelled. "I need help."

A woman's voice answered, "Who is it? What do you want?" It was a voice that seemed shaky with age—or was it fear? But no woman had cause to be afraid, not on Ariban.

"I am Colin, son of Fergus and Hedda, of Merton Town. One of our sheep is mired in the lake."

The door swung open and he found himself looking down at a small frail-seeming woman, the top of whose head barely reached his shoulder. She looked up at him, nodded a silent greeting, and listened as he spoke.

"You'll need rope," she said abruptly, and vanished into the darkness of the cottage, returning a short time later with a coil of rope in her hands.

"The ladder's there, against the house." She gestured, and Colin hauled it down and put it over his shoulder, holding out his other hand for the rope. But it seemed she was coming too, since she slung the coil over her shoulder and wrapped a shawl around her. She didn't wait for him, but set off with brisk strides along the verge of the lake. *Not so frail after all. And independent*, he thought.

"There she is." Colin pointed when they reached the spot. The ewe had continued to struggle since he had seen her last, and now, although her front legs were still hanging across the tussock, her back end was even more deeply mired.

"That'll be a job. My ladder's barely long enough."

"Needs must. It'll have to do." Colin tossed the ladder from him so that it lay along the surface of the mud. It fell short of the sheep by a good arm's length. The woman uncoiled the rope and silently handed him the loose end. He fastened it in a loop around one wrist, flung himself flat onto the mud so that the upper part of his body was lying along the ladder, and began to edge slowly forward.

From the first he was terrified. With every movement he could feel the ground quake and heave beneath him, and he imagined himself sinking beneath the mud. Imagined it flowing into his eyes, his mouth . . . He dared not move too fast. There was a stink of decay that made him gag. As soon as Patch saw him she valiantly tried to struggle free, succeeding only in getting more deeply mired and sending mud spattering over him.

It seemed an eternity before Colin reached the end of the ladder and stopped to wipe the mud and sweat from his face. Now, when he stretched out one arm, he could just touch the muddy fleece of the ewe's back. He wriggled closer, so only the lower part of his body, from the hips down, was safely borne by the ladder.

"Take care!" the woman cried from behind him.

He grunted a reply, loosened the rope from around his wrist, and began to push it painstakingly down into the mud beneath the ewe's belly.

It was agony. With his arms extended in front of him, his upper body had no support. If he were to relax for an instant and allow his body to fall forward, his elbows would sink into the mud and he would be as helpless as the stupid sheep. With his right hand he groped under the sheep's belly for the free end of rope. The mud was clammy like cold porridge. *Where* was that rope end?

There. He pulled it through, made it tight around the main rope and, with a groan of relief, wriggled back until he was able to rest his chest on the ladder again. He lay there for a few breaths, his head turned to one side away from the mud, while the muscles in arms and chest throbbed agonizingly and his back felt as if it were broken. He wondered if he would ever again have the strength to move.

"Are you all right? Shall I come out and help?"

"No, don't do that. I'm fine." He took a deep breath, clawed a tiny piece of courage and energy out of nowhere, and slowly began to wriggle back along the ladder until his feet touched solid ground. He felt her arms, surprisingly strong for so small a woman, hauling on his legs, pulling him back, until he could finally stagger upright. The relief was unbelievable. He stretched his knotted muscles and sucked in deep breaths of clean air, rejoicing in the simple fact of being alive.

Patch gave a bleating reminder of work yet to do,

and he twisted the rope around his hands. "Here, let me help." The woman's hands grasped the rope, and together they leaned back and pulled. At first there was no response but a frantic bleating. Then, with a horrible sucking sound, the mud let go and the ewe was skidding on her back towards the shore along the rungs of the ladder, her legs stiffly in the air.

"I hope I haven't broken her back," Colin gasped, muddy rope hanging in slack coils from his hands. He had never felt so tired in his life.

"There was no other way you could have got her free, lying the way she was," the woman said practically. "Come, let her stay as she is. The ladder will make a good litter so we can carry her back to the cabin. Then we will see what a pailful or two of water will do for her."

They set off with the ladder between them, the ewe lying limply along it like a muddy hearthrug. Once back at the cottage, the woman fetched a pail of water and poured it slowly over Patch, tenderly washing out her nose and mouth, sluicing down her wool. Before long the ewe gave a plaintive bleat, scrambled to her feet, and stood there, shaking quantities of muddy water all over them.

The woman laughed. "Fine thanks, you wretch!" She offered Patch a handful of greens, which were quickly whisked out of her hand.

"She'll be as right as rain now, I reckon," the woman said. Then she looked at Colin and laughed again. "You look as if you could stand some of the same treatment. You'd best come and get washed and fed."

Colin looked down at himself, his jerkin, shirt, and breeches caked with shining mud, and mud oozing from his shoes. "I won't come in and soil your house. Give me a pail outside. That'll do me fine."

"You're no sheep, lad. You deserve better. Come. I was planning on a bath myself, so I've hot water on the stove. Strip off those clothes outside and I'll find something clean for you."

He took off his shoes and socks and dropped his shirt and jerkin to the ground. As he stood awkwardly, still in his breeches, she laughed. "I'd a boy almost your size once. Many a time I scrubbed his back for him. But don't fret. I'll keep my back turned till you're safely in the water."

She hurried into the cottage, and he could hear the sound of water being poured into a metal tub. He clambered awkwardly out of his mucky breeches, which clung to his legs, and ventured inside. A metal tub stood invitingly in front of the peat fire; he climbed in, grateful for the sting of hot water against his chilled skin.

"Here's a jar of soap and a towel, then." She placed them on the floor beside the tub and turned to open a chest standing against the wall.

"And when you're clean and dried off, you'll find a pair of clean breeches and a shirt that I believe will fit you well enough. Now I'll leave you in peace and go rinse off those clothes of yours."

Alone, Colin looked curiously around the room. It was smaller than his parent's home, with a bed pushed against one wall, the chest against the other. Beside the fireplace was a cupboard for storing food and dishes, and in front of it a table and two roughly made chairs. There was no man's gear lying about, and he guessed that she must be a widow. Apart from several bundles of herbs hanging from the ceiling, the room was empty and unadorned. A sparse, poor place, though spotlessly clean. But its owner's kindness, he thought, was ornament enough.

He concentrated on scrubbing his body, washing his caked hair, and getting the mud out of his ears. After ducking for a final rinse, he climbed out of the tub, wrapped the towel around his waist, and went over to the chest. The breeches the widow had laid out were well made and, though worn, had been neatly mended. He wondered if they had been her husband's. He tied the cord of the breeches around his waist and pulled the shirt over his head. It was well woven and, like the breeches, as good as new. There was also a pair of woollen socks, finely knitted. When he pulled them on, he found that they were a little short in the toe, made for someone with a smaller foot than his.

Colin swung open the door, hauled the tub out, and emptied the muddy water over the vegetable plot that she pointed out in front of the small cottage. He rinsed the tub and restored it to its place on a nail on the wall inside the cottage and then went out to where the woman was watching Patch.

"Thank you for your kindness—for saving Patch's life. My father will be most grateful. Now we must be on our way."

"You cannot leave without a bite to eat," she protested. "I have washed your shoes and they're drying in that last patch of sun over there."

Colin tried to protest, but she waved his objections aside. "Patch is dining." Indeed he saw that the ewe was contentedly grazing as if nothing were amiss. "You must also. Now, come in. I hope the clothes fit well enough."

"Thank you. Yes, indeed." He followed her back into the tiny cottage and watched while she put out bowls and spoons, ladled broth into the bowls, and put a half loaf in the centre of the table.

"Sit. Sit and eat," she urged him. The soup was cheeringly hot, with a good herbal taste, though, having no meat in it, it was thin compared with the soup that Hedda served. Colin wondered again why this woman should live alone, apparently so poor. That was not the way Ariban treated its widow women.

The bread was excellent, and he broke off a generous hunk to eat with his soup. He was reaching for a second piece when it occurred to him, with embarrassment, that perhaps she had no more. He drew his hand back, his cheeks reddening.

"Take more, please," she urged. "It is good to see a young appetite."

"Thank you for your kindness, but Mother will expect me to eat supper when I get home and . . ." He improvised. "If I can't finish every scrap, she will think I am sick."

She laughed then. "Very well. I will not press you, though you need not worry. I have enough. My neighbours see to my needs." Her mouth twitched in a small bitter smile, and again Colin wondered at her situation. He got to his feet, and she let him go reluctantly.

"I will come back with the clothes you lent me," he promised, taking from her the bundle of his own damp clothes.

"I look forward to seeing you again," she said. "But as to the clothes, they are of no use to me. Keep them, I beg you."

"Thank you," he stammered. "You have been very kind."

There was a pride on her face that stopped him from suggesting that he should pay for them. *But perhaps there is something I can do to help her around the place*, he thought. *A woman alone. Far from her neighbours.*

He whistled to Patch, who was loath to leave her lush new pasture, and set off back towards Merton Town, swinging wide to the northwest so as to avoid the edge of the lake, lest the silly sheep should take it into her head to look for another meal of bog moss.

The sun had set, and the moon was hanging bright in the southern sky, halfway betwixt empty and full, by the time he reached home. He had left Patch on the grazing grounds with the rest of the flock. The family were already at the supper table, and Hedda looked up anxiously as he came into the house. "What kept you so long?" his father asked. And Hedda added, "And what is that you are wearing?"

"I had quite an adventure. But Patch is safe, Father,

though somewhat muddy, as are my own clothes." He dropped the damp pile at the door, sat down at the table, and recounted his adventure.

"How kind," Hedda exclaimed. "I must give her something in return."

"I think she is very proud, Mother. But perhaps you could spare one of your blankets. I noticed that there was but one on the bed. And only a half loaf of bread."

Hedda frowned. "How strange. The folk of Lynn usually look after their own, as we look after ours. Tell me again, exactly where was her house?"

Colin explained in more detail. He had hardly finished when Fergus pushed back his chair and got to his feet with an exclamation of anger. "Are you fated to bring us into disrepute, my son? First you bring us all this trouble with the Stranger here, and now you meet the one person in the whole of Ariban who is accursed. I wonder at you, boy! Really I do!"

Colin's mouth fell open. Praise he had looked for, not blame. His cheeks grew hot and his hands doubled into fists. "You bade me go find the missing ewe, Father, and I did, mired to her shoulders in the bog, as I just told you. Without the widow's help, she would have died. Then she succoured Patch and bathed and fed me. What do you mean—she is 'accursed'?"

Hedda put a soothing hand on Colin's arm. "Hush, boy, your father doesn't mean—"

"But I do, Hedda. I do. Could you not have guessed who she must be, boy? Living alone, far removed from Lynn-by-the-Lake?"

Colin shook his head.

"Aileen, the mother of Alan. That is who she is. And you entered her house, broke bread with her . . . If Elder Shepherd should hear of this!"

"He will *not* hear of it," Hedda put in soothingly. "No one in this house will speak of it, Fergus."

"And you will not go there again," Fergus ordered, frowning at Colin.

"But I have the clothes she made and the socks she knitted. You said you would give her a gift in exchange—"

"There will be no gift-giving. Your mother will wash the clothes, and I will return them secretly and leave them on her doorsill."

"It seems most unfair," Colin burst out. "Fine thanks to her for helping save Patch!"

"That is enough. Since when do children criticize their fathers? Since the Stranger came into our midst, nothing has been as it should!"

Colin shot a glance at Jennifer, who had sat silently throughout this conversation. Now she raised her eyes and looked at Fergus. "If visiting the mother of Alan will bring suspicion on your house, perhaps you will let me go. Nothing worse can be said of me than has already been said."

Fergus's mouth fell open. "Well . . ."

"No, Fergus, that would not be right," Hedda said quickly.

Fergus raised a hand to silence her protest. "It is an idea worth considering, Hedda. She can slip away secretly. No one will talk to her or offer to accompany her. The shepherds do not go north of Lynn

Lake, and the villagers of Lynn-by-the-Lake will not see her."

"But if the Elders *should* hear of it, it would be added to the list of her sins. Is that fair? Would you tell him that you permitted her to go?"

"He will not have to," Jennifer interrupted. "I will go of my own free will, and secretly, as you suggest. Only the socks Colin wore are muddy from his shoes. I will clean them now and fold the other clothes. If a blanket and a loaf of bread should happen to be left out overnight, I will take them too. I will go before sunrise, and no one in Merton Town will be a whit the wiser."

"Aye, it's a good plan, wife." Fergus put a hand on Hedda's shoulder, as if it were she who had been talking and not Jennifer. "See to it."

CHAPTER SIX

"You'd better stay out on the grazing grounds today," Fergus grumbled to Colin the next morning. "That'll keep you out of mischief."

It might keep him out of mischief, but sitting with nothing to do but look at the sheep grazing and whittle a spoon from a piece of driftwood left Colin at the mercy of his thoughts. In spite of himself his eyes kept wandering to the north, towards where Jennifer should reappear. She had left at first light, as she had promised, with the bundle containing the clothes of the widow's husband wrapped in a small woven blanket, and with a loaf of bread tucked into the bundle. The journey should not have taken her long, but by noon she had still not returned.

He looked up once more and noticed that Patch, the silly ewe, was grazing closer and closer to the northern edge of the pasture. If he didn't watch out, she would get herself mired in the lake again, and then Father would really be angry. Colin headed her back to the centre of the flock and, sitting on a hummock where he could keep an eye on her, unwrapped the cloth that held his lunch.

While he was munching on his crusty bread and the smooth tangy cheese Mother had made, Jennifer appeared suddenly in front of him. She must have come from the western track, not from Lynn-by-the-Lake, or he would have seen her approaching. Her hands were doubled into fists and her face was white with rage. In the ten days he had known her, he had never before seen her as angry as this.

"Where is it? What have you done with it?"

"Huh?" For an instant he didn't know what she was talking about, his mind still on the widow Aileen and her dead son, Alan.

"My story box. Where have you hidden it?"

Her brilliant eyes flashed accusingly, and Colin felt his cheeks grow red. "It's—it's mine by right of salvage," he blustered. "I told you that before." It had felt like a good argument when he had used it to justify his hiding of the box. Now it seemed thin and weak.

"You did not rescue either it or me from the sea, hero boy. We were already ashore. My hand was on the box. It is mine."

He had no answer. He tore off a piece of bread and chewed it, gazing at the sheep, pretending to ignore her. She stood in front of him, glaring. The bread stuck in his throat and he struggled to swallow it.

"*Please.*" Suddenly her voice was soft, persuasive. "Give it back, I beg you."

"Why? It's no use to you here on Ariban, is it? And if they decide to run you off the cliff, it will be no use to you then." His voice broke into sudden gruffness. Putting it into words made her execution seem possible, and horribly real.

"I won't wait here to be driven off a cliff! I intend to escape before then. But I must have my box back. What use is it to you? Give it back to me, I beg you."

Colin flushed again and stared at the sheep so hard that they became a white-grey blur in front of him. Patch could have escaped and he would never notice. He was conscious only of the girl standing in front of him and of his heart pounding in his chest.

The box *was* hers. He should give it back. But, even though it did not contain jewels or gold, its importance to Jennifer gave his possession of it a kind of power over her, something he had not yet worked out. He might "discover" it again, and take it to the Elders. Surely they would be impressed with his honesty, and he—and his family—would no longer face dishonour.

On the other hand, once the Elders saw that it contained evil books rather than precious gems, they would be angry and more inclined than ever to condemn Jennifer. The cliff? And death? He bit his lip. What was he to do?

"Oh," she exclaimed, frowning. "You think the box may be the price of your family's safety, do you not? That's clever of you, Colin, but I wonder if it is wise."

"I don't see the difference," he said roughly.

"Being clever will solve your problem—the problem of *me*. But can you live with the result of that decision for the rest of your life?"

"Bargaining my family's safety against an old box?" He gave a forced laugh. "I can live with *that*."

If only that is all I have to live with, he thought, trying to harden his heart against her. *She's my enemy, not my friend*, he told himself firmly. *She has bewitched little Etta, and because I found her on the beach I must face the Moot.*

"I want to tell you a story." She sat down on the grass beside him.

"I don't want to hear it. Stories are lies, and lies are evil."

"No. Remember: the lie is a truth," she answered quickly. She smoothed her homespun skirt over her knees and began to talk softly, her eyes no longer fixed on him, but on the distant horizon. In spite of himself, Colin found he was listening, the words spinning a subtle net, drawing him in.

"Once upon a time, not so many years ago, there was a fisherman. He had his own small boat that he named *Wind Runner*, of which he was very proud. He also had his own cottage and a wife whom he loved and a son who would one day grow old enough to help in running the boat, hauling in the nets—a son who would take some of the weight off his shoulders as he grew older. Like the other fishermen around him, he was contented with his lot.

"His son became old enough to sail with him, to learn the ways of the sea, rather than staying home with his mother, drying fish and mending nets. Proudly the fisherman took his young son out to sea. But in front of his eyes a terrible thing began to happen. He saw that his son was afraid. The sea, which to the father was not only his livelihood but also a friend and companion, was to the boy an enemy. The fisherman argued with his son. Day after day he took him out in *Wind Runner*, trying to accustom him to the sea, but day after day the boy became more terrified, even though he tried desperately to hide his fear from his father.

"Then the boy began to dream. Fearsome dreams in which the sea crept up to the cottage, lapping at the door, seeping in through the shuttered windows until, at last, his bed would float out of the cottage on the floodwaters, swirling round and round until he and it were sucked under the waves. He would wake up choking as if he were really drowning. Now, whenever his father sailed with him to the fishing grounds, he would begin to choke and turn blue, because he could not get his breath.

"Full of disgust that his only son was a coward, the fisherman once again left the boy at home with his mother. Too proud to ask one of the other men in the village to sail with him, he went out alone. One day a sudden storm swept over the fishing grounds and the fleet turned to run for home. They all got back safely except for one man: the fisherman who was alone, who had no one to help him.

"Though his mother never uttered a word of blame, a feeling of guilt grew and grew inside the boy. And the dreams returned, worse than they had been before, so that he would wake not only his mother but the neighbours with his screams.

"The village Elder called the young man and his mother in front of him. He listened to their story and to that of the accusing villagers. The young man was told that dreams were evil and that he must stop them at once. He laughed bitterly. 'I would that I could,' he told them. 'But I am haunted by the sea. I know that one day it will be the death of me.'

"The Elder ordered him to leave the village and never return, so he kissed his mother good-bye and went sadly to the big town to try to earn his living there. But it was hard. As in his own village, every man and woman had his and her appointed task, and there was no place for a stranger to fit in. Again the dreams began to haunt him. Whispers and sour looks followed him down the streets. Finally the Elders of the town listened to the people's complaints and decided to end the evil, once and for all.

"They voted to get rid of him and drove the boy across the grazing lands and to the top of the mountain that overlooked the sea."

She paused in her story. Colin stared at her, his mouth open. "Alan. You're speaking of Alan, who was thrown off the cliff top into the sea," he stammered.

Jennifer nodded. "His mother, Aileen, told me that they did not have to throw him down. At the last he looked at her and smiled and said, 'Finally I am free.' Then he jumped. As he had foretold, the sea was the end of him."

"But I thought, from what Mother and Father said, that the people of Ariban had actually killed him. Well, the truth is not so bad after all, is it? And it was all a long time ago."

"But the people of Ariban *did* kill him, if not with their hands, then with their thoughts and intentions." She sighed. "Yet healing him would have been so simple."

"I don't believe you. If it were possible to cure Alan of his fears, I know the Elders would have found a way. We are not brutes, Jennifer."

"No, only ignorant. He died because the people of Ariban denied his cure."

"Which was?"

"To speak of his dreams. To understand that dreams are a window into the inner life of the person. To learn the truth of that inner life and accept it."

"But his father had only one son," Colin interrupted. "He had every right to demand that his son sail with him."

"Were there not families in Lynn-by-the-Lake with more than one son whom they could lend to Alan's father to raise as a fisherman, learning his trade, inheriting his boat?"

"I've never heard of such a thing," Colin said, annoyed.

"In many countries where I have travelled, sons— and daughters too—are adopted into other families so that they may learn new skills and new ways of life. So, for instance, a child with a talent for music might be sent to a great house or a palace to learn to develop these talents. Or a storyteller, like myself, would live with other tellers and learn their myths."

"Weren't you lonely, away from your family?"

Jennifer shook her head. "All tellers are in my

family, and all listeners my friends. I was never lonely until I came to Ariban."

"Mother and Father took you in. Etta is your friend—too much your friend for her own good," Colin blustered.

"And you, Colin?"

He opened his mouth and then closed it again and swallowed. *The box.* Always it came between them. Quickly he changed the subject, back to their original discussion.

"Alan was the son of a fisherman. He was bound to fish. These are our ways."

"The ways of Ariban!" Jennifer sighed. "Do you not *see* that if Ariban had stories, there would be a story for Alan's father, so that he would not grudge his son a life on land?"

"That's all very well. But what about Alan? He feared the sea and failed his father. What story could you tell to comfort *him*?"

"Not to comfort," Jennifer corrected, "but to teach. Perhaps one like this . . . There was once a prince," she began, and Colin realized with surprise that this was the story he had read. But it changed as it went along, and this time the prince was attacked by frightening spirits until, in the end, he learned that the life of a prince was not the right life for him—that he must face his father, the king, and bid him farewell for ever.

"I know that story," Colin exclaimed. "But the ending is different."

She looked at him sharply, paused, and then said, "Every story is different, as every life is different.

The skill of the storyteller is in fitting the story to the listener. Which means knowing what the listener needs." She stopped, and then laughed. "You have listened to two different stories in the course of one afternoon, and you are unharmed. You haven't grown donkey's ears, nor have I turned you into a seal or a merman."

"Of course not. We don't believe that kind of foolishness."

"Then why are you so afraid of story?"

"We're not afraid—"

"What do you think will happen to you?"

Colin suddenly found himself remembering the time when he was very small and had been trapped between the shearing-shed wall and the door by a very angry ram. Cornered and afraid.

"N-nothing. It's . . . it's our law, that's all. It's always been that way."

Jennifer nodded and sat silently for a while, absently pleating the hem of her skirt. Then she closed her eyes and touched the fingers of her left hand to the fingers of her right. She opened her eyes again and looked straight at Colin. He blinked at their brilliance.

"I have one more story. May I tell it to you?"

He wanted to listen, and at the same time he didn't want to hear what she had to say. *She is like a spider*, he thought. *Her stories are webs, spun to catch me as the story of the prince caught me.*

Wanting to hold those hands, to look into those eyes, he jumped to his feet. "I am tired of your stories," he lied. "Why should I listen? Anyway, I am supposed to be watching the sheep."

He walked rapidly away, north towards Lynn Lake. And thought of Alan. He hesitated and turned. Jennifer was standing still, her hands held out towards him. He walked slowly back.

She sat down on the grass and smiled up at him. "Come. Sit. There is no one to hear but you and the sheep. And the sheep care only about their own story. Now listen . . .

"Once, long ago, but not so long ago after all, there was an island in the western sea that was far removed from the commerce of the rest of the world. But, though isolated, the island was famous for the quality of its wool and the skill of its spinners and weavers, so ships began to sail into its harbour to trade for woollen goods.

"When the sailors went ashore, they boasted, as sailors are wont to do, telling tales of other ports they had visited and the curious and fascinating things they had seen in other lands. These stories were told and retold, growing ever more elaborate, as stories do when left to themselves. Soon the young men and women of the island began to say to each other, 'Why should we stay here at the edge of the world, with nothing to look forward to but tending sheep and spinning and weaving wool, or fishing and drying the catch?' And they began to leave the island.

"Then the older people became concerned. 'What will happen to us if all the young people go? If we have no grandchildren to look forward to, life will become meaningless. The island will die.' So they decided that no longer would foreign sailors be allowed ashore to infect the young people with their tales. 'All this nonsense will soon be forgotten,' they told each other.

"But it did not happen as they had hoped, because the stories that had already been told were becoming part of the fabric of the island. The young people grew up believing that out there, far beyond the horizon, were a thousand cities whose streets were paved with mother-of-pearl and amber, and they were restless, wanting to go and see for themselves. So then the Elders forbade the telling of these stories. They were lies, the young people were told. And lies are evil.

"Strangely enough, this still did not put a stop to the problem. When the telling of stories was forbidden, the idea of a wonder-filled world beyond the horizon began to become part of the dreams of the young ones. 'We must forbid dreams,' the Elders decreed. But forbidding was not enough. Every human dreams. Even dogs dream."

"You're wrong," Colin interrupted. "I don't dream. Mother and Father don't—"

Jennifer shook her head. "Indeed you *do* dream. But you have been taught to forget. So now the only dreams that the children of Ariban remember are the nightmares from which they wake in terror. Like the drowning dreams of Alan. Like the monster dragons of Etta."

"But this is only a story. You're not really talking about Ariban, are you?"

"It is a story—and it is true."

"How can you possibly know? You were not here. And even if what you say *is* true, it must all have happened long before any of us were born."

"Storytelling is the retelling of forgotten history. I see this island today, and so I know what all the yesterdays on the same island must have been like. This retelling is a kind of healing, like the wise woman's herbs." Jennifer looked straight into Colin's eyes. In the same tone of voice she went on. "My box contains healing, and you must give it back to me."

He jumped at her sudden demand and had no reply ready. His head was still spinning from her story. *Could it be true?* He shrugged. "What makes you think I have it?"

"Because you have read one of the tales in it: the story of the prince. You recognized it and knew that I had changed the ending."

"If you have all these stories in your head, why do you need the books?"

"Don't your fishermen have charts of the waters around Ariban, even though they must know the hidden rocks and shoals by heart? And your mother has a book of recipes, as well as patterns for her loom, though she, too, must know the threading and treadling by heart. The story books are like recipes, like patterns and charts. They were given to me by my mother, Irvette, who got them from *her* mother, Godiva, who got them from *her* mother. And these books are only copies of older books that were written right back in the beginning times. When I have my books, I know I will not run aground on a rock of forgetfulness, nor thread the yarn of my story through the wrong heddle."

"Why are you sitting idly, talking of weaving? What business is it of Colin's?" Gwynne's sharp voice behind them made them both jump.

"How guilty you look, the two of you!" she went on, her little eyes darting from one to the other. "Maybe it was not weaving you were talking of, but something very different—something evil."

"You startled me, that's all," Colin said. "Creeping up on us like that."

"Why should you be startled if you have nothing to hide? You have nothing hidden, have you, Colin?" Gwynne questioned him mockingly, and he flushed with guilt, wondering if she knew that he had hidden the story box. But how could she? She did not even know that it existed.

"As for you, Stranger . . ." Gwynne turned on Jennifer, her voice as full of spite as a wasp is of poison. "Hedda sends me to tell you that you are needed back at the house. She wonders why you have tarried so long. You had better make haste."

Jennifer stood up gracefully and shook the creases from her skirt. Without a word she passed Gwynne and walked quickly back towards Merton Town, leaving Colin and Gwynne together.

Gwynne dropped down to the grass beside Colin and began to fan herself with her sunbonnet. "How warm it is today! It will soon be summer." Her voice was now as sweet as honey, very different from the biting tone she had used towards Jennifer.

"Yes. We are to start shearing this week, Father says." Colin answered her automatically, his mind still occupied with Jennifer's story of Ariban.

"And after shearing comes the Midsummer Festival."

"Of course. It is less than a month away."

"You haven't forgotten that at Midsummer we will be married?"

How loud her voice is, compared to Jennifer's, he thought. "Of course not. You spoke of it the other day, on South Peak." But he *had* forgotten, the whole time Jennifer was telling him stories. She *was* a witch. She must be.

"Yes, I did. On Sunday afternoon, before you went running off to Half-Moon Cove. You have spent a lot of time there recently. Almost as if you had a secret."

"What nonsense you do talk, Gwynne. You know I had the salvage rights," he said defensively. Through his mind ran the opening lines of the story he had read. *Once there was a young prince . . .* In *that* version of the story, the prince travelled the world and finally came home to take up the duties he was destined for. Was that to be the ending of *his* particular story? To be married to Gwynne? To raise sheep? Yes, of course it must be. Any other kind of life was unthinkable.

But . . . *I know it was Gwynne who persuaded Colleen to get Etta into trouble, and make matters worse for the whole family. Why did she do it? Out of spite?*

"My grandfather, Elder Fisher, is worried about our marriage." She interrupted his thoughts, and for an instant an unexpected relief flooded him, leaving him speechless. Gwynne went on awkwardly, apparently taken aback by his silence. "Things have changed, Colin. You brought this Stranger into our midst, a person who has upset our way of life, told lies—it was you who brought her here, remember."

"I can hardly forget, when I think of what I stand accused. My possible fate," he added bitterly.

"It is a pity. I reminded Grandfather that it *was* you who saved Irving and his boat, and that you are a hard worker and a good provider. I told him that it was because you were the first out after the storm to claim salvage that you found *her*."

"Her name is Jennifer," Colin said coldly.

"I know that. What a strange, foreign-sounding name, to be sure! Anyway, Grandfather said he must abide by the decision of the Moot. If you and your family are cleared of any wrongdoing, our marriage will go ahead as planned." She got to her feet and shook out her skirt. "I have work to do. I can't waste time sitting gossiping—even if others can."

"But, Gwynne," he said slowly, "do you not understand that if the opinion of the Moot goes against me, my life is forfeit? What of our marriage plans then?"

"Hush. That will never happen. I am sure of it." But she bit her lip, and Colin wondered if she was sorry now that her spite had led her to betray Jennifer and their whole family.

"It is what the widow Nola wants. Two lives for two lives."

"I am sure my grandfather will dissuade her. The Stranger's life, perhaps, but never yours. It is laughable. But still, think about what I have said, Colin. If the marriage between us is forbidden, it will be because you are proven to be a troublemaker. If that is so, everyone will know of it, and you will not be likely to find a wife anywhere on Ariban. So take care. Keep away from the Stranger."

There is another world out there, thought Colin, as he watched her walk briskly across the grazing grounds towards Merton Town. *A great world of which I know nothing.*

On the other hand, marriage to the granddaughter of Elder Fisher is not to be sneezed at. And these stories of Jennifer's are only that, after all—stories.

He stood up and walked restlessly among the sheep. *If her stories are true, people of Ariban once left the island to explore that world. Maybe I can go too, like the prince in the story.*

Nonsense! He shook his head. Jennifer had trapped him in her story web. *No, Gwynne is right. I must be on my guard. And she will make me a good wife. Father will help us build our own cottage, and once we are married, half his flock will be mine. We will have a fine life here on Ariban. And, after all, who cares what the rest of the world is really like?*

An impulse almost sent him running after Gwynne, to tell her he cared nothing for Jennifer. But something held him back. He needed time to make sense of the fable that was—and was not—the history of Ariban. Could it be true? How could she—a foreigner—possibly know things about his own island that he had never even heard rumoured?

CHAPTER SEVEN

Over the evening meal Colin found himself watching Jennifer. Her face was pale, and he couldn't help noticing that the hand holding her spoon trembled suddenly, so that a drop of stew splashed onto the table. She put down her spoon and looked at Fergus and Hedda.

"I am sorry for the trouble I have brought to your family. It is poor thanks for rescuing me from the sea. I wish there were something—"

"Wishes don't clip the sheep nor spin their fleece," Fergus interrupted her, his voice harsh. "You should have kept your wicked thoughts to yourself." He reached for another piece of bread to soak in his stew.

Colin saw his mother's mouth open. Then she pressed her lips tightly together and swallowed. "Would anyone like more stew?" she asked, instead of whatever she had intended to say.

Colin shook his head.

"I'm not hungry." Etta laid down her spoon. Her lip was quivering.

Hedda sighed. "Off to bed with you then. Both of you," she added, looking at Jennifer but not using her name.

Colin saw a glance pass between the two girls, as if early banishment to bed was what they wanted. *A chance to talk secretly*, he thought. Etta was definitely bewitched and, if she wasn't careful, she would get into as much trouble as he. The thought flashed through his mind: *I should listen to their secret talk. I don't trust the Stranger.* He told himself that it was for Etta's sake and not in the least because he was jealous of Jennifer's spell over his little sister.

He watched them climb out of sight, got up from the table, yawned, and stretched. "I'll have an early night too," he said casually. "Good night, Mother; good night, Father."

He untied his shoes and went up the ladder in his socked feet. The curtain separating his room from Etta's was already closed, and he tiptoed over to it and squatted on the floor. He could hear Jennifer's soft accents clearly.

". . . so I cannot stay in your house any longer. Every day my presence here puts your family in danger."

"You *can't* leave, Jennifer. Whatever will I do without you?"

"Come, Etta, little one. A moon ago you had not even known of my existence. If a moon from now I am gone, what difference will it make to you?"

"All the difference in the world. You are my friend. And, oh Jennifer, what if my dreams come back?"

"You know what causes them. You can change them with stories of your own. You can be strong all by yourself."

Etta's voice was vehement. "I *need* you."

Colin heard Jennifer sigh. "I will be of no help to you if you are run off the cliff or if you are flogged to rid yourself of your so-called sin. You will be better off without me. I have found a place to hide before the Elders hold their Moot. I think that once I am gone, they will no longer blame Colin. But before I go, I must find my story box. It is the whole of my inheritance. If only I knew where he has hidden it!"

"I wish I could help you, Jennifer."

"Perhaps you can. I know that Colin found my hiding place and hid the box somewhere else so that I should not discover it."

"I'm sorry I took your key. I shouldn't have. . . ."

"Don't grieve over spilled milk, child. I know he has found the box and read one of the stories. But I don't believe he would dare bring it back to Merton Town unless he were intending to take it straight to the Elders, and this he has not done. So it is still hidden in the cove. Isn't there some place you know of—some secret cave, perhaps, that you and Colin discovered when you were small?"

"Colin is much older than I am, so we seldom played together."

"I suppose not. But think—did he tease you, hide things from you?"

"Why, yes!" Etta's voice went up. She continued

in an excited whisper, and Colin had to strain his ears to hear her words. "I had a doll baby that Father carved for me from a piece of driftwood. Mother made clothes from scraps and even knitted a tiny shawl. Colin hid it, and for days he wouldn't tell me where it had gone. Then at last he showed me the place. It was a little cave with a shelf above the entrance. I remember he lit a torch and took me into the cave and said, 'Your doll is in here. If you find it, you can have it back.' And I looked everywhere, even digging in the sand, while he watched me and laughed and laughed. Then he said, 'Why, you're as blind as an egg, Etta.' Then he reached up and pulled it off a ledge above the entrance. I couldn't see that high then. I was quite small. Isn't that strange? I had forgotten all about it. But now I remember. Oh, how angry I was with him!"

Colin bit his lip. He remembered hiding Etta's doll. He even remembered the pleasing surge of power he had felt when she could not find it. Yet he had been a grown boy, and she was only a baby. How stupid he had been! As a result of his childish teasing, Etta knew his secret. Now Jennifer was talking again, asking Etta if she remembered where the cave was.

Be quiet, he wanted to shout at her. *Don't you dare tell!*

"Could you find it again?"

"I think so. But how can we go to the cove without being seen?"

"Could we pretend to gather seaweed—that is a thing you do, is it not?"

"Not the two of us alone. Girls and women of

133

Merton Town don't wander off by themselves. The only times I have been to Half-Moon Cove are when we've all been gathering sea birds' eggs or dulse."

"Then we must go when we will not be seen. What if we were to slip out at dawn, the way Colin sometimes does?"

"It would be broad daylight when we returned, and we would have to explain where we had been."

"Then we must go at night and return while it is still night. That would be possible, wouldn't it?" Jennifer's voice was brisk, and Colin could see her firm uptilted chin in his mind's eye.

"No one *ever* travels at night."

"Then there is less chance of us being discovered. Tomorrow the moon will be four nights from full. It will rise in the late afternoon, so even after sunset we will be able to see our way. There is no wind, and the morning sky was clear today. The weather will hold."

"I could never find the right place without light— not in the dark. We will have to take a tinderbox."

"Leave that to me. And, Etta, do not be afraid."

"I am not so *very* afraid. But perhaps I could persuade Colin to give *me* the box," Etta suggested. "Then we wouldn't have to go to the cove in the dark after all."

"You could certainly try. But don't let him know that I intend to escape the island. I don't quite trust your brother, Etta. He has not yet grown enough to know his own path."

"His path? What does that mean? And he is truly good, Jennifer. And kind. He never teases me anymore."

Colin heard Jennifer's faint laugh. But all she said was, "Go to sleep, child. We'll worry about what to do in the morning."

Seething with anger, Colin went to bed. *Stupid* Etta, giving away his secret! Jennifer's fault, of course. She wound Etta round her finger like a strand of wool. Take back the box? He would soon put a stop to that. He'd run to the cove next morning and get the troublesome box himself—take it to Elder Shepherd and have done with it.

"Colin, I have a big favour to ask." Etta followed her brother out of the house early the next morning and caught him by the sleeve.

"Yes, little sister. What is it?"

"Jennifer's box. Please give it back to her."

Colin frowned and shook his head. "You don't know what you're asking, Etta. I have a plan to get us out of trouble, and I need the box."

"But it is *hers*!" Etta's voice rose.

"Shh." Colin looked anxiously around, but it was early yet and the cobbled street was all but empty, except for three women gossiping down by the well. "I know she's put you up to this. You don't under-stand, little sister. Jennifer is the enemy of the people of Merton Town—indeed of the whole of Ariban. She cannot claim the box. It is mine."

Etta's lip began to tremble. Anytime now she

would start bawling, and he would be in deeper trouble. Colin thought quickly. "Here, you may keep the key for me." He slipped the thong from his neck and dropped it over Etta's head. "There now."

"The key is not the same as the box, and you are treating me like a baby!"

"Etta!" Hedda's voice came from inside the house. "What are you doing out there? Come in at once where I can keep my eye on you. As for you, Colin, have you forgotten that shearing starts today?"

He *had* forgotten. So much for retrieving the box and giving it to Elder Shepherd. He hurried to the grazing grounds to start bringing in the sheep.

The rest of the day passed in paddocking the sheep, hauling them, one by one, under Fergus's nimble shears, and then driving them, skinny and snow-white—save for the single patch of dye that marked them as Fergus's—back to the grazing grounds.

"Oil the shears and hang them in their place," Fergus ordered at the end of the day, straightening slowly, his hand to his back.

"Next year you should let me do more of the shearing, Father," Colin said without thinking. Then he caught his father's eye, and the silent thought passed between them—*next year, will we still be together, father and son? Well, the Moot will decide*. Colin gave a forced laugh. "Of course, next year Gwynne and I will be married. I shall have my own flock."

"So you will, son," said Fergus heavily and turned towards the house. "So you will."

Colin took his time cleaning and oiling the shears. The sun had almost set when he left the shed, and the side and rear of the house were rosy-red in its light. He found himself staring at the familiar scene, devouring it hungrily, as if he would never see it again: the beauty of Ariban, of his home. Then he told himself not to be foolish and walked towards the door.

I'm starving! I could eat three bowls of stew, I swear. He stopped on the threshold. Something was wrong. Different. He walked back and stared at the whitewashed western wall, painted with all the colours of the setting sun.

The ladder! Every house in Merton Town had its own ladder, propped against the thatch at the rear. Every storm brought damage and the need of repairs to the reeds and ropes. Only constant vigilance and care kept the inside of the houses dry and secure in the face of gales and driving rain. *Now the ladder had been moved.*

He walked past the house and looked up casually at the south side. Sure enough, there, propped under the window to Etta's room, was the missing ladder.

So Jennifer was serious in her wild plan to rescue the box that night. But what then? She had told Etta she had found a place to hide until Midsummer brought the foreign fleet to Merton Harbour. What did she intend to do with Etta after the box was found? Abandon her at the cove? Surely not. She would bring Etta safely home and *then* escape with her precious box while it was still dark.

Could he go ahead of them to the cove and get the box? Tell her she was too late? While he still hesitated, the door opened and Hedda called, "Supper is on the table, son. Don't keep us waiting."

And the moment was lost.

During supper he was aware of a fidgetiness in Etta—a kind of spark and excitement different from her usual docility—and he wondered that their parents did not notice. But Fergus was wrapped in silence, partly habitual, partly from the exhaustion of shearing, while Hedda moved automatically from hearth to table, serving out bowls of stew, laying out loaves of fresh bread.

She spoke only once, in a flat voice. "I took my bread down to the ovens this morning, and not a soul greeted me, coming or going."

Fergus raised his eyes from his bowl. "It will pass," was all he said, his voice heavy. Colin felt more than ever the weight on his shoulders of all he had done: rescuing Jennifer, persuading his mother to shelter her, concealing the story box.

What he must do was suddenly clear to him. He must follow the girls to the cove and allow them to retrieve the box. Then he would take the box and Etta, and leave Jennifer to find her refuge, wherever that might be.

I will have the whole solitary way home to talk sense into Etta, where her shrill voice cannot tell the whole of Ariban how she was involved, he plotted. *I must persuade her that her friendship with Jennifer is too dangerous, that she must be silent.*

But the box. What of the box?

I will take it directly to Elder Shepherd and tell him that I overheard Jennifer's plan to escape. I followed them to the cove in order to discover where this box was hidden. Then I snatched Etta and the box and came directly to you, Elder . . .

Yes, it will work, he thought, pleased with himself.

As soon as supper was finished, Etta and Jennifer went upstairs. Colin helped his mother clean the bowls and pot, and then he, too, went upstairs. He did not undress, but slipped off his shoes and lay on his bed, listening to the silence, watching the shadows creep across the room.

At length he heard the squeak of a shutter. He lay, motionless, his eyes a slit, as the curtain between their rooms twitched.

"Good. He is asleep. Now, quiet as a mouse, little one. I will go first and guide your feet on the rungs. Don't be afraid."

In the silence that followed, Colin counted to fifty, then crept to his window and pushed the shutter wide. In the moonlight he could just see the two shadowy figures passing the last few cottages. He took shoes in hand and climbed out of Etta's window after them.

At the foot of the ladder he paused, looking south towards the centre of Merton Town. Not a light burned. Not a shadow moved. It was all right: they had not been observed.

He turned and followed the other two, keeping a fair distance behind, since he knew exactly where they were going. They set a slow pace to accommodate Etta's short legs; occasionally Colin had to stop lest he get too close. He could sometimes hear Etta's shrill voice on the still night air and Jennifer's answering murmur, though they were too far away for him to catch the words.

Probably telling more stories, he thought, wondering at the ease with which Jennifer had captured the affections of the shy Etta. *Lies and deceits*, he told himself. Etta had always been more withdrawn than other children of her age and, in recent years, Colin had been her only real friend. Now all that had changed.

He paused, looking back over the grazing grounds towards the dark shadow of Merton Town. Then he stared and rubbed his eyes. *Is that a light?* He waited, staring past the moonlight and the shadows, but the spark was not repeated. He turned and saw that the two girls had reached the top of the zigzag path leading down to the cove.

"What's that behind us? That shadow?" Jennifer's voice was suddenly clear. He froze.

"Just an old sheep." Etta's voice. "Listen to the waves down there. How loud they are in the darkness!"

Then they were gone and Colin moved again, approaching the edge of the cliff until he, too, could hear the voice of the hungry tide and, over it, the occasional clatter where one of them kicked a pebble off the path into the black emptiness below.

He crouched at the cliff top and saw a small spark where Jennifer struck steel against flint. He saw the dried moss glow and catch a piece of bark, then a stick, the flame licking its tip. He saw Jennifer swing it to and fro until the flame grew strong. Now he could see their shadows below him, dancing grotesquely across the beach.

Then the shadow of the smaller figure ran up the beach until it grew large against the cliff face. Etta's shrill voice was borne up to him on the breeze. "It's here. Jennifer, bring the torch close. Yes. See, you have to duck your head and wriggle to the right. There is a little passage, and behind it the cave. It's as secret as secret can be."

She vanished, and Jennifer, holding the flaming torch, vanished after her, leaving the beach in darkness. With no need for caution, Colin took the downward path. At first he hurried, but he had never come here at night before. As the path turned and twisted, he glimpsed the sea far below, glinting silvery-white in the shifting light of the moon. Then, suddenly, he would be in darkness, wary of roots that could trip him and send him hurtling over the edge. Then, once more, brilliant moonlight, outlining every stone and root.

It seemed an eternity before he reached the shore and the shifting smooth pebbles of the upper beach. The tide slid in and out, rippling over stones, washing the sand with moonlight. He ran up the beach to the entrance of the cave. In the half darkness of the entrance passage he crouched, his heart pounding so loudly that he was afraid they might hear it.

Etta's voice echoed sharply in the cave. "You'd never guess, would you? See, hold the torch high. I'm still not tall enough to reach, but by next year I'll have my own hiding place here."

"What will you hide?" There was laughter in Jennifer's voice.

"Why, I don't know. But it will be here if I need it."

"That is always a good thing. Hold the torch, child, while I lift the box down and unlock it."

There was a silence, broken by a gasp of wonder.

"*Books!* How beautiful they are. I have never seen books like these. But then, I never *have* seen books except for Mother's recipes and pattern books. And the Book of Rules, of course. Only six? Can six books really contain all the stories in the world?"

Colin heard Jennifer's laugh and imagined her lovingly touching the ornamented covers of each book. "There are as many stories in the world as there are rivers flowing to the sea. But just as each little stream becomes a river and flows into the ocean, and then is sucked up by the sun and falls as rain to renew the stream, so each story comes from and returns to the same source. It is changed, but it is the same. So you may find in this one book the source of all the seeking-wisdom stories—stories such as the one your brother found and read."

Colin heard Etta stammer, "I-I was wrong. I shouldn't have taken your key."

"Do not be concerned about it. Who knows? One day that story may be important to him."

"And the other books?" Etta prompted.

"Here are the stories about Sorrow. And about discovering Self. In these books are stories of Forgiveness and of Remembering. And here are stories about Courage—"

"That's the one you told me," Etta interrupted. "Is the monster I dreamed of in this book?"

"It and many other monster and dragon creatures. The story I told you is only one of a thousand tributaries joining the river that flows into the ocean of story. These six books hold the wisdom of the world." She sighed. "Now I must put them back, take the box, and leave. It is time, too, for you to go. You must hurry if you are to get safely back to Merton Town and into your bed before moonset."

"What do you mean, 'time for *me* to go'? Aren't you coming home with me first?"

"I am not." Jennifer's voice was suddenly grave. "This is the crossroads where our paths must part."

Colin had overheard her plan. He knew what she intended, but it had not truly become real until now. He felt as if a hand had taken hold of his heart and squeezed it. It was hard to breathe. *Where will you go, Jennifer?*

He heard Etta echo his unspoken question. "But where *can* you go?"

"Oh, Etta, I told you I must leave Ariban before I bring more trouble to you and your family."

"But the foreign fleet won't be in until next full moon. Where will you go?"

"Hush. No more questions, dear Etta. If you don't know my plan, then you can't give it away to—"

"I wouldn't. You *know* I wouldn't."

Colin heard Jennifer sigh. "I know you would never willingly betray me, Etta. But the Elders are much more powerful than you are, dear girl. If they can destroy the memories of dreaming, they can certainly pick one small fact out of a child's brain. Believe me, my way is the wisest. Some time in the future, at a moment that seems good to you, you must remind Colin of *his* story. Of the search for wisdom. Come. It is time to leave. You have the torch. Will you lead the way?"

As Colin slipped from the entrance passage, he

heard Etta cry out, "I will never forget *my* story: The princess set forth with her magic sword to conquer the dragon."

Jennifer's laughter followed him. "Yes, dear child. And always remember that there are many kinds of dragon and many kinds of battle. But you will win, because you have the sword of courage. Now let us be on our way. We will say our last good-bye at the cliff top. Then you will go south, and I east."

Colin's mind raced. *I'll stand to one side. Grab her when she comes out. Take Etta and the box safely home, just as I planned. I will tell the Elders that Jennifer forced Etta to come to the cove for the box. And then . . .*

He tested his lies to see that they would work, but it was not until he turned and saw the line of torches dancing in the breeze that he realized, with a lurch of dismay, that his story was useless. The people of Merton Town had followed them here—how had they known?—and he and Etta were trapped in the cove, along with the foreigner, Jennifer, and the box of books that would surely seal their fate.

One last desperate plan flashed into his mind. Jennifer was truly fond of little Etta. If he could persuade her to give herself up, to take the blame . . . He ducked back into the passage, the flames of Etta's torch full in his face, almost catching his hair alight. As she gasped, he pushed her back towards Jennifer, who stood, box in hand, within the cave itself.

"See what you've done," he whispered, whipping himself into righteous anger, not far removed from the fear that actually gripped him. "The whole town is outside. You'll surely die now. And you'll have brought the same fate on Etta. Did you think of *that* when you dragged her out here?"

Jennifer's eyes widened in horror. Even in the golden light of the torch he could see her face grow pale. She swayed, and instinctively his hand reached out to steady her.

He heard Etta wail, "*Die? We're not going to die, are we?*" and he hardened his resolve.

"Not if I can help it." He snatched the box from Jennifer's hands and grasped Etta firmly by the wrist. "I'll tell them you forced Etta here, that I followed you both and rescued her from you. Do you understand?" She nodded, white-lipped. He pulled Etta's arm and she struggled against him. "But it's *not* true. She's my friend. I was helping her."

"Hush, Etta. Not a word. You'll ruin everything." He wanted to say something to Jennifer. Something about what he felt . . . how sorry he was that . . . if only things had been different . . . But there were no right words and there was no time. He had no choice. The crowd outside had taken that from him.

He turned away and pulled Etta from the cave into the dazzle of torchlight that swallowed the stars. *These are my friends. The friends of my father*, he told himself firmly. *They are not our enemies.*

He shouted above the sound of the waves and the voices of the crowd. "Thank the Almighty that you've come! She's in there. I've just rescued my little sister from her clutches."

It should have worked. He could feel the mood of the crowd change. But then Etta tore her wrist free and ran down the beach, among the gathered men, waving her torch like a sword.

"Run, Jennifer, run!" she screamed. As the men turned to chase her, she threw the torch recklessly from her. It landed among them in a shower of sparks and a curse or two, as the hot wood found a mark.

"Grab her!" someone shouted.

There was another curse. "The little witch bit me!"

"Got her!"

"Don't hurt the child. This was none of her doing." The voice was quiet, but everyone turned. There was a sudden stillness, such as happens at the turning of the tide. Jennifer stood by the cave entrance, tall and straight in the flickering torchlight.

Instinctively Colin grabbed the chance. "I have her!" He caught her arm. "And her precious box too." She didn't move as his fingers bit into her arm.

Beyond the crowd he saw Etta's face. She said nothing. She didn't have to. *Traitor*, her eyes told him. *My own brother has betrayed our friend.* He tried to outstare her, but he could not. His eyes dropped.

Jennifer was hustled from his side. He turned away, his own face as stiff as stone. As he followed the triumphant crowd up the path, a voice inside his head said, *Once there was a prince . . .*

But the story is not supposed to end this way, he thought miserably. Then he straightened his shoulders and took a deep breath. It was only a story. A lie.

It's for Mother and Father, as well as for Etta, he told himself. *I'm doing it only to save our family from contamination. And there are no princes on Ariban.*

CHAPTER EIGHT

The sky was aglow with pre-dawn light when Colin found himself, not at home, but sitting at the table in Elder Fisher's house. Opposite him sat the Elder, and the troublesome box with its shining brass straps and hinges lay on the table between them. By the fire knelt Elder Fisher's old wife, a shawl wrapped around her shoulders, coaxing the peat fire into life. In the shadows behind the fireplace stood Gwynne.

Why is she here instead of at home in her bed? Colin wondered resentfully. *Hasn't she meddled enough already?*

On the long tramp back from the cove, he had asked one of his neighbours how they had guessed that Jennifer planned to escape. The man had laughed. "Gwynne saw the Stranger move the ladder to the side of the house last evening. She wondered why and told her grandfather." He had nudged Colin in the ribs. "You're to marry her at Midsummer, aren't you? You'll have to watch out, married to a smart one like her. No climbing out of windows for you!" He had slapped his thigh, Colin remembered, and laughed immoderately.

Colin clenched his fists. *Gwynne has betrayed us again, as she betrayed Jennifer and Etta the day after the storm. Out of spite, because she saw that I was happy talking to Jennifer.* He realized how foolish he had been not to understand before that in her own way Gwynne was as dangerous as Jennifer.

"The box is locked." Elder Fisher's words interrupted Colin's thoughts.

"Yes. She—" Colin stopped. He must not be seen to know too much. "I expect she has a key," he added quickly. "Shall I go home and demand it of her?"

"Home? You will not find the Stranger there. Nor your sister either. They lie in Merton Town jail, where they belong, safe from further mischief. No, Colin, son of Fergus, you will stay right here, where I can see you clearly. Gwynne will go for the key. If it is not on her person, Granddaughter, you will go to the house of Fergus and Hedda and search the house from floor to thatch. Do not return without it."

"Very well, Grandfather." Gwynne tightened her shawl around her shoulders and slipped silently out of the house.

The room was quiet except for the faint *huff-huff* of the bellows. Elder Fisher did not shift his piercing gaze, a gaze that seemed to shrivel Colin into nothingness. He dropped his own eyes and stared at the box, the source of all his trouble. If only he had not been greedy. If only he had taken it at once to Elder Shepherd, a more gentle, less shrewd man. If only . . .

Colin's head spun with weariness, with the telling of lies patched together with the truth, with the effort of trying to remember what he had said before. And now he felt as if a stone were lying on his chest. Etta and Jennifer in jail! He had failed to protect his little sister. And he had trapped Jennifer. That was the worst.

Elder Fisher's interrogation had been ruthless, seeking out every weakness in his story.

"How did I know the Stranger had taken Etta? I heard them climbing out of the window, so I followed."

"Why did you not warn your parents of what had happened?"

Colin had hesitated. There were so many possible paths, so many lies. Which was the best? "I was afraid for the honour of my family, sir. Already we were in trouble, through no fault of our own. I hoped I could stop them before it was too late."

"But you failed to catch up with them. Surprising. With your strength and longer legs, I would have thought . . ."

Colin was still wracking his tired brain for a reply when the Elder went on. "Why did you suspect Etta was not going of her own free will? Did she struggle or cry out?"

He had shaken his head numbly, and then remembered the box. "I hoped to follow them to Half-Moon Cove and recover her treasure. I knew Jennifer—the

Stranger—had hidden it previously. I had seen it when I rescued her but, when I went to look for it later, it was gone. I guessed the Stranger had taken Etta to guide her back to the cove, so she could get her hands on her precious box again. That is why I followed her."

"You never mentioned this box before, neither to your parents nor to us. Your whole story smacks of deceit, boy."

"It was to be a surprise," he had blurted out. "I hoped to please Gwynne and you by presenting you with a great treasure. That is what *she* called it. *A treasure far richer than gold or jewels.*"

The Elder's hand had been on the box. He had sent for the key . . .

How long Gwynne is taking, Colin thought desperately.

The Elder abruptly broke the silence. "What are you really about, boy? Where do your loyalties truly lie?"

He jumped. "Why, with you, sir. With Merton. With Ariban."

The old man was silent, and Colin found himself babbling, though he knew that it would be wiser to hold his peace. "It wasn't my fault that I found her in Half-Moon Cove. And it was Craig and Blair who carried her from thence to Merton Town."

"You were very pleased to have her stay with your family, were you not?"

"I-I suppose I was. After all, she was like salvage—like the timber I brought home. I thought she would be useful to Mother."

"You weren't thinking of yourself, then? The Stranger—she is a beautiful woman, is she not?"

Colin shrugged, his face flaming. "What was her face to me, Elder Fisher? I did not think of her that way. After all, I am to marry your granddaughter, Gwynne, at Midsummer."

The room was silent again. The Elder's wife quietly placed bowls on the table and filled them with warm goat's milk. Then she set a loaf of bread in the middle.

The Elder grunted an acknowledgement, broke a piece of bread, and soaked it in the warm milk. He gestured for Colin also to eat, and Colin's spirits rose slightly. Surely the Elder would not break bread with him if he suspected him of being an enemy of Ariban? He dunked his bread and put it in his mouth, but even softened with milk it was hard to swallow.

Perhaps this also is a test, he thought, and almost gagged on the mouthful. He got it down, his eyes watering, and followed it with a second piece. All the time the Elder's eyes were on him, boring into him, seeming to read his mind.

He gave a sigh of relief when at last the door opened with a bang. "There was no difficulty, Grandfather," Gwynne said triumphantly. "It was fastened around her neck." She laid the brass key, still threaded on its leather thong, on the table in front of Elder Fisher.

"Sit, girl. Sit." He waved her to a chair. "Let us all see. Who knows, perhaps you may have a share in this Stranger's wealth!" His voice was biting, and Colin felt his cheeks get hot.

The Elder pulled the box towards him and slid the key into the lock. Gwynne leaned eagerly forward, and Colin saw the eyes of Elder Fisher's wife flash in the firelight as she, too, watched. He doubled his hands in his lap, his nails biting into the palms. *If only it were really gold or precious stones*, he thought. *The Elder would be happy. Gwynne would receive a splendid bride-gift. And I . . . I would be reinstated as a hero.*

The Elder turned the key and slowly lifted the lid.

I must remember to be surprised, Colin thought. *As surprised as they are. But not too soon.* He tried to imagine the box filled with golden doubloons, with shining pearls and bright stones.

"*What!*" Gwynne's shrill voice broke the silence.

"I don't understand," Colin stammered. "She said it was full of treasure." *Not gold and jewels. Treasure far richer than gold or jewels, she had said. What had she really meant? They were only books, after all.*

The Elder said not a word. He tipped the box so that the six books slid onto the table. The lamplight shimmered on the golden edges of the pages, on the jewel colours cunningly inlaid into the tooling of the leather covers. Elder Fisher picked up the first book, riffling through its pages with a careless thumb, shaking it, and then letting it fall to the table. It fell open at an illustration of a dragon, shimmer-scaled in blue and green, flames curling from its fiercesome jaws.

The Elder slammed shut the book and put his hand over it, almost as if he believed that the ferocious monster could escape. He drew the other five towards him and placed them in a neat pile, his gnarled hand on the topmost.

"I will study these abominations with my brother Elder," he said sternly. "Then we will bring our findings to the Moot. The people of Merton must decide what is to be done with the Stranger and the child Etta. As for you, Colin, son of Fergus, you will go home and say nothing of this discovery to your parents or to anyone else."

"Yes, Elder Fisher." Colin got to his feet, thankful to escape. He hesitated. One more chance, perhaps, to make good. "Elder Fisher, the box . . . it is a good box and finely made. I wonder if . . .?"

"You want to claim it as salvage for yourself?" The voice was biting. "Indeed, you do not miss an opportunity, do you, young man? Well, it is a fair claim. We shall see." Despite his courteous words, the Elder's grey eyes were like stones.

"I do not ask it for myself," said Colin quickly. "But as a bride-gift for Gwynne."

"Hmm." The sharp eyes softened. "That also will be considered. Now be off. You too, Granddaughter."

Colin saw another small way of repairing matters. "May I see Gwynne home first?"

"Yes, yes, I suppose so, though I dare say she knows the way well enough. Remember, you are to say nothing of this, either of you. You have seen *nothing*."

"No, Grandfather."

"No, Elder Fisher."

The sun was already rising ruddily above the horizon, and Merton Harbour lay below them in a pool of rose as they silently left the house.

Gwynne put her hand on Colin's arm. "There is something I must tell you before you take me home."

Colin saw that her cheeks were red. Her eyes dropped, avoiding his. "It was I who saw the Stranger place the ladder below Etta's window yesterday. It was I who told Grand-father and suggested he have your house watched."

Colin swallowed. *Here was another test. Another step further away from Jennifer and towards Gwynne.* He did not tell her that he already knew. Instead he said, trying to make his voice approving, "That was very observant and clever of you."

"You are not angry at me?"

"*Angry!* Why would I be angry? I am proud of you, Gwynne. You did what was right for Merton Town. For Ariban. If only . . ." He paused, thinking of the right words that could be turned to his family's advantage, for he knew she had a lot of influence on Elder Fisher—indeed, she was his favourite grandchild.

"Yes, Colin?"

"If only the Stranger had not influenced Etta. It is unfortunate that they were so close all the time, sleeping in the same bed as if they were sisters, working together every day. But of course none of us suspected . . . I believe that the Stranger must have put a spell on Etta. Otherwise she would never have gone away with her."

Gwynne tucked her arm into Colin's and walked with him slowly down the cobbled street towards her father's house. "That's true, Colin. And your sister is very young, after all. Perhaps I may be able to persuade Grandfather."

He squeezed her hand. "That would be a good and just thing to do."

He left her at her father's door and walked up the hill towards his own house, on the whole pleased with what he had done in the face of apparent disaster. *Being a prince in a story is all very well*, he told himself. *But this is Ariban. This is the place where I must live, the place where I will marry Gwynne at the Midsummer Festival*. So, when the memory of the brilliant blue of Jennifer's eyes returned to haunt him, he pushed the image firmly out of his mind.

But when Colin sat with Fergus and Hedda in their place on the slope of the moot ground two days later, after Sunday meeting, it was hard indeed to forget the colour of Jennifer's eyes. They were fastened on him. So bright, so blue. But they were not accusing. It was almost as if she understood him—which was even more unbearable, because he still did not fully understand his own motives. It seemed to him that he was being sucked into one disaster after another, like a man mired in a bog.

As for Etta, it was obvious that the poor child had spent much of her time in prison in tears. Her eyes were red and her face swollen. But she was not crying now. She stood beside Jennifer and held her hand tightly, looking at the same time brave and pathetic.

Part of Colin longed to run across the moot ground

and hug her, free her from this Stranger's grasp, and bring her back to her own family. The other part of Colin stayed still and small, hoping not to be noticed. Sitting between his parents, he felt his father stiffen and heard his mother give a stifled sob. But they did nothing either. They sat like obedient sheep waiting for the Elders to speak.

The moot ground was in a small dell just to the north of Merton Town, and normally it was used only once or twice a year, when the foreign ships came to Merton and the price of the fine Ariban wool, in pots, pans, nails, and other barter goods, was decided upon. This Moot was different. Colin could only vaguely remember one other like it, long ago, before Etta was born. The air was full of a tingling excitement, like the feeling before a lightning storm. The hair on his arms prickled and, in spite of the sunny day, he shivered.

The two accused stood on a small natural platform, known as the Judgement Stone, that thrust itself out from the short turf. Elder Fisher stood on the one side and Elder Shepherd on the other, while the slope opposite was crowded with all the people of Merton Town—men, women, and children, shepherds and fisherfolk. A gentle breeze swept across the moot ground, sending the shadows of small clouds scudding over the meadowland.

Elder Fisher moved forward and raised his gaff. The murmur of conversation died instantly and a tense silence fell over the crowd. "People of Merton Town," he began in the age-old formula, "we have come together at Moot in response to a danger that threatens to destroy the very fabric of our existence, that mocks our whole way of life. Listen and judge."

Elder Shepherd now came forward, raising his crook and showing it to the assembly. In his soft voice, which still carried clearly across the moot ground, he began to speak. "This crook is like the staff you shepherds use to guide your sheep. It is a stick with which you can tap the flanks of your ewes to guide them in the right direction. It is hooked at the top so that a shepherd can catch a sheep that is in danger, can haul it from a crevice or from a bog. Sometimes a shepherd's crook may seem like a weapon, but it is not. Its purpose is to be guide and helper—as it is today, for among our flock a sheep is lost, is in peril, and we must labour to put this matter right.

"How did this come about?" he went on. "It is not for nothing that we forbid merchant seamen to come ashore at Merton Harbour. It is not for nothing that we allow no strangers into the precious land of Ariban. But in spite of our laws and our precautions, a Stranger has come among us, brought here through no wrongdoing but by wind and wave. Not brought wilfully, it is true, but yet kept among us through the misjudgement of some of our own folk."

Colin saw every head turn towards him, every eye pierce him, and he felt his cheeks burn. But the fear that threatened at times to grip him loosened its iron bands. If he understood Elder Shepherd aright, he and his family were being accused of little more than stupidity. He took a slow, steadying breath and looked up, boldly returning the accusing eyes of his neighbours.

Now Elder Fisher spoke in his turn, his voice harsh and accusing. "Brother Shepherd," he said, bowing formally, "you speak with justice, but with perhaps too much gentleness towards your own."

Elder Shepherd inclined his head. "Do you judge differently, Brother?"

"I would choose, rather than judging, to put Colin, son of Fergus, to a test of his loyalty, if you permit."

Colin's heart thumped violently. Hedda caught his arm in her hands and squeezed it so tightly that later he was to find bruises there. His father's face did not change. It was as still and as hard as if carved in stone.

Elder Shepherd nodded. "So be it. Colin, son of Fergus, are you willing to accept the verdict of my brother, Elder Fisher?"

Colin stood, pulling his arm from his mother's grip. He tried to stand tall, but his knees trembled and his voice was more like a mouse's than a man's. "I am willing, Elders."

"Then step forward into the middle of the moot ground."

The people in front parted willingly to let him through. In fact it seemed to Colin that they were eager to move away, as if even his touch or his shadow might contaminate them.

He walked steadily down the grassy slope to the bottom of the moot ground and up the farther side until he was standing below the Judgement Stone, the top of which was level with his chest. Unless he tilted his head, he could see only the robes and sandalled feet of the two Elders. He chose to stand respectfully, head bowed, his eyes on a clump of yellow star-flowers growing in the turf at the edge of the Stone. He had no desire to meet the eagle eye of Elder Fisher.

At the Elders' feet was Jennifer's treasure chest. The old man stooped and lifted it from the ground. As he held it aloft, the sun glinted brightly on the brass straps. Colin could hear the murmur of curiosity that ran through the crowd like wind through the grass.

"This box was brought ashore by the Stranger and hidden by her, which proves her ill intent. It is filled with evil things—evils that in your name I now reject." As he finished speaking, Elder Fisher turned the box upside down so that the books fell to the ground at his feet in a cascade of colour, of gilt edges and illuminated pages.

It does look like a treasure, Colin found himself thinking, remembering with a stab of regret the greed that had made him discover Jennifer's hiding place and then hide the box himself. If only he could relive that stormy day. If only he had gone straight to the Elders with his story of the Stranger. If only he had handed over the troublesome box then. If only . . .

Elder Fisher was speaking again. "The evil of the Stranger crept among us, contaminating our young people. If it were not for the vigilance of my granddaughter, Gwynne, it might have continued to flourish unseen, causing untold harm." He paused dramatically, his eyes sweeping the silent crowd, before he continued. "Colin, son of Fergus, I accuse you of bringing this trouble among us. The Stranger was washed ashore in the dark of the moon. Tonight the moon will be full, yet you only brought the box to me two nights ago. I am still amazed that you did not bring it to us sooner."

Colin opened his mouth, a ready excuse on his lips, but Elder Fisher raised a hand to silence him. "Words will no longer serve, Colin, son of Fergus. Actions alone will prove your fidelity to the ways of Ariban. Take this tinderbox. In the middle of the moot ground you will see the makings of a fire. You will light it."

Colin bowed and looked around. A rough circle of stones marked the place. There was tinder and kindling to make a fire and a goodly pile of timber heaped beside it. His hands trembled so that he had to strike the flint a dozen times before making a spark that would ignite the tinder. When the spark finally caught, he held the smouldering tinder close to his mouth and blew it gently into life. Then he placed it among the small pieces of wood at the heart of the fire. Once it had caught, he looked up at Elder Fisher for guidance.

"Build it up well. This is not a peat fire merely to keep the hearth warm. This is a flame to cleanse all of Ariban."

Colin obeyed the Elder, piling on the wood, remembering with bitterness the last time—the only time—he had made a fire like this. But then it had been to restore life. This time . . .

His heart thumped and his mouth was as dry as dust as he built up the fire carefully, piece by piece, until flames licked blue and green over the salt-soaked wood and its heart grew hot and glowing. What had the Elders in mind? Death by fire? No! That was impossible. It was not the way of Ariban. And he told himself firmly that though it was a fine fire, it was by no means big enough to burn a witch.

A bony finger beckoned him close, and he walked reluctantly forward until he was standing directly below the Judgement Stone. Again he faced the Elders. Etta stood just behind them, clinging to Jennifer, staring at him accusingly.

In Jennifer's face he saw a flash of understanding—and horror. Her eyes closed. He saw her take a deep breath. She opened her eyes again.

Don't look at me like that, he wanted to beg her. *Do you not see that I cannot help myself? That I must do whatever I am told?*

Elder Fisher held out his hand, and Colin returned the tinderbox. Their hands touched. The Elder's was cold and dry. Like a snake's skin.

"Now you will pick up the evil books and show them to the people of Merton. Then, one by one, you will tear out every page—these pages filled with lying words and lying pictures—and you will burn each one in the sight of us all."

"Colin, you can't!" It was Etta's shrill voice. She pulled her hand from Jennifer's and stepped forward recklessly, her hands outstretched. Jennifer did not move, but Colin had to wrench his eyes away from the pain in hers. *I'm sorry. I have to do this thing.*

Elder Shepherd hooked the end of his crook around Etta's neck and quickly hauled her back. Colin was afraid of what she might do next, but Jennifer leaned forward, caught Etta's hand, and drew her close to her side. Her sobs and the crackling of the fire were the only sounds Colin could hear. The whole assembly sat silently, waiting.

"Do it!" Elder Fisher hissed, and Colin meekly picked up the first book, showed it to the crowd and then, page by page, tore it apart, letting each page flutter onto the fire. He saw the dragon writhe in the flames, so that for an instant it seemed to come alive, breathing real fire, before it was consumed and fell into blackened ash.

The leather cover dropped from his hands to the ground, and he picked up the second book and destroyed it too. He saw a young man on horseback set out on his quest. A maiden spun straw into gold and another lovingly caressed a fearsome beast. And so, book by book, on to the sixth. As the last shards of paper shrivelled among the hot embers, he laid the six leather covers on the flames.

When it was all done Colin stood upright, facing the Moot, the judgement of the people of Merton Town. The smell of burning leather was repulsive, quite different from the clean smell of burning paper, and he gulped, suddenly nauseated.

In the silence a skylark rose from the grazing grounds behind the people, soared into invisibility, and then plunged back towards the ground, singing its heart out. He had the fanciful thought that perhaps the skylark was the soul of the books that he had destroyed; that though he had destroyed the pages, maybe the *idea* of the books might still be alive. It was a comforting thought. But it was only fancy. He knew bitterly that what he had done was dreadful and could never be undone.

He took a deep breath and turned to face the Elders.

"Well, Brother?" Elder Shepherd challenged Elder Fisher, and the latter nodded his head.

"Colin, son of Fergus," he said, "you have passed the test, and we declare you innocent of all but carelessness and stupidity. For that we can blame your youthfulness. Go now. Return to your place with your family."

This time, as he made his way through the crowd, Colin's neighbours nodded and smiled, as if to say, "Forget the way we acted before. We knew you were innocent all the time."

But I'm not, thought Colin, as he hunched over in his place on the hillside, his head bowed to his knees. *I don't know why, but what I just did feels worse than what I was accused of.*

He sat between Hedda and Fergus and, with all the people of Merton Town, watched the fire burn the covers of the books. A line of dark smoke rose from the embers to foul the clear blue sky. Finally Elder Shepherd ordered a man sitting close by to fetch a pail of water, douse the fire, and then kick apart the blackened embers.

Only when this had been done and the man had returned to his place did Elder Fisher speak again. "My brother Elder and I have thought long and hard about the Stranger. Her evil books no longer exist. They can do no harm. But what of the Stranger herself? We can keep her in prison until the merchant ships come with the next full moon. But if we send her away with them, what is to prevent her from returning? It seems to both of us that the only way to keep our precious island safe from further contamination is by removing her as finally as we have removed her evil books. The lies in her evil books have gone up in smoke. But what of the lies still in her head and her heart? How can we be sure that they will no longer harm us?"

Now Elder Shepherd stepped forward and spoke. "We are equals here on Ariban. Each man and woman over the age of twelve has a vote in the assembly of the Moot. You may cast it as you will, but remember: this vote is both our freedom and our guilt. Do we choose to send the Stranger away on the next merchant ship, or do we drive her over the cliff into the sea?

"Each of you will take a pebble from the basket, either a white one or a black. Hold it secretly in your hand until the bag is passed to you. Then drop it in. Remember this, that white is for her life and black for her death. Choose well and wisely."

The people shifted and looked uneasily at each other. The older among them were aware of the process; many must be remembering Alan of Lynn-by-the-Lake. But to Colin and the other young people, this was a new and terrible ritual.

The basket was passed along the rows and each person in turn picked a small pebble and held it securely in his or her hand. Life and death, Colin thought, as he looked in the basket. What an awesome responsibility. Then he consoled himself with the thought that his vote was only one among a hundred and fifty or so. It was nothing. It didn't count. But . . . His mother nudged him. His hand closed over a white pebble and he passed the basket along.

When the woollen bag was in turn passed along the line, he slipped in the white pebble he had chosen. Even if it made no difference in the end, his guilt would be less.

When at last everyone had voted, the two Elders tipped the heavy bag onto the bare rock in front of them and began to count. It took less than a few heart-beats for them to tally the result. "Three white. The rest black. People of Merton, you have chosen that the Stranger die. Let your judgement stand. The Stranger will be thrown from the top of South Peak into the sea at sunrise three days from now." Together the Elders struck their staffs of office on the bare rock. The sound echoed hollowly across the moot ground.

Colin saw Jennifer sway, her hands go to her mouth. He longed to reach out and hold her in his arms, tell her it was all right, that it was not true.

But it was.

Three white. Only three. Were the others Father's and Mother's? Or someone else's? He would proba-bly never know. But it was not important. *Jennifer will die. Will be gone as if she had never been.*

Elder Fisher's voice broke through his thoughts. "Two lives for two. Now we must pass judgement also on the child, Etta. My brother Elder has pleaded for her on the grounds of her youth, that as a child she is ignorant of the damage she has done to Ariban, that the Stranger has influenced her unduly, and so on. I too have received similar pleas."

So Gwynne did as I asked, thought Colin grate-fully. *If they all think like this, Etta will be safe*. He looked up hopefully as Elder Fisher went on.

"He is very persuasive, but I have brought forward an argument that he has not been able to counter. It is this, people of Ariban. If a sheep gets the mad sickness, it must be destroyed—even if it is a ewe lamb—lest the sickness spread to the rest of the flock. We have a sick ewe lamb among us. I argue that we must vote as we voted before. The question is the same. Is Etta, daughter of Fergus, to be banished from Ariban forever? Or is she to meet the same fate as the Stranger who contaminated her? Choose your pebble, people of Merton, and vote."

"This is too harsh a choice, Elder." Hedda was suddenly on her feet, her voice shrill in the sudden silence. "She is a child, not a sheep. Let the vote be for forgiveness or banishment, not banishment or death. Let not the history of Ariban be marred by yet another death of an innocent young one. Those of you who are old enough to remember, I charge you, look into your hearts as I speak the forbidden name: Alan of Lynn-by-the-Lake."

A sigh rippled through the crowd as if everyone's breath had been suddenly drawn in at the mention of that name.

Elder Fisher's grey face flushed angrily, and he raised his gaff high. But, before he could lower it in judgement, another woman cried out from the assembly, her voice echoed by yet another.

"She speaks as a mother, Elder."

"Aye, forgive her words and have mercy, Elder."

"Not death for a young one. Not again."

Elder Shepherd leaned forward and whispered to his brother Elder. For what seemed like an eternity the two grey heads bent together. At last Elder Fisher nodded grimly, and Elder Shepherd lifted his crook. "Mercy shall prevail on Ariban. Let the question be this: Is Etta, daughter of Fergus, to be forgiven or banished?"

The women cheered, and so, too, did a few of the older fishermen. Hedda collapsed onto her knees, sobbing with relief, and Colin put his arm round her. *How brave she is to stand up for Etta*, he thought. *Much braver than I.*

Once again the pebbles were chosen and cast into the bag. Once again the bag was tipped out upon the Judgement Stone. But this time the vote was much closer. The Elders had to separate the pebbles into two piles and count each of them twice before they came to a decision. It seemed to Colin, though, that the black pile was a little larger. His heart sank. How could his sister survive banishment to a strange land? Without family? Without protection? With no skills but the simple homely ones of chopping vegetables, drawing water, and carding wool? In the end perhaps death might be the more merciful judgement.

The Elders spoke, and the crowd was silent. "People of Merton, this is the final judgement of you all: seventy-eight in favour of banishment, seventy-three in favour of forgiveness. Etta, daughter of Fergus and Hedda, you will be sent from Ariban on the first ship arriving here at the next full moon, never to return."

The crowd stirred uneasily. It had been done and could not be undone. The silence was broken by Etta's wail, "What will become of me, Jennifer? What shall I do?"

Colin saw Jennifer hold Etta close in her arms and saw the unshed tears that made her eyes even larger, more brilliant. She whispered to Etta in a voice too low to be heard by the assembly. Colin read her lips and knew, because she had spoken the same words before, what she said. "You will go forth with your magic sword of courage, child. Do not be afraid."

CHAPTER NINE

In the main room of their cottage, Hedda and Fergus
sat in stunned silence, each of them mourning alone
the sentence that had been passed on Etta by the
Moot. Colin had tried, stumbling over his words, to
comfort his parents, but they had turned their stony
faces from him. Always silent folk, their affection
implied rather than spoken, they had no skills with
which to meet this final disaster. Nor had they any
comfort for him.

Now, in the darkening attic above, Colin crouched
by the window, the empty story box on the floor
beside him.

No rats lived on Ariban, but occasionally one
would escape off a visiting merchant ship, scamper-
ing down the mooring rope to shore, and would have
to be trapped. Colin had seen one of these creatures,
kept in a cage for the amusement of the fisherfolk of

Merton Town. He could still remember how it had scurried round and round in its cage, turning back and forth until, at last, it had fallen exhausted to the floor.

This was precisely how his mind felt now, as his thoughts raced round and round. Round and round. It was *his* fault that Etta was to be exiled. It was *his* fault that Jennifer had been condemned to a violent death by being thrown from Ariban's South Peak. If only he had left her unconscious on the beach for the incoming tide to take kindly, gently, without fear and violence. If only his greed had not led him to hide the story box, and his cowardice persuaded him to "find" it again. If only he had had the courage to defy the Elders and refuse to burn the books. There were enough "if onlys" to fill all the days of his life with dusty regret.

He glanced at the little box, with its neat brass fittings, its well-made corners, and the soft leather washer between box and lid that made it watertight. Even looking at it nauseated him. What devious thought had made him ask Elder Fisher for the box? Why had he said he would give it as a bride-gift to Gwynne? Right now he wished he could take the hateful box to the top of the cliff and throw it into the sea. Be done with it. But he had *not* done that, and now it would be among Gwynne's possessions to remind him, for the rest of his life on Ariban, of his stupidity, his greed, and his cowardice.

He groaned and buried his head in his hands. *Once there was a young prince* . . . He had never behaved like that prince. Not once. Even the rescue of Irving had been an unthinking act of bravado, rather than true bravery.

Was it too late now? If he *were* a prince, he would order the immediate release of Etta and Jennifer. But their sentence was not the choice of the Elders alone, but of the people of Merton Town, voting in the Moot as they had done in centuries past. How could he contradict their wishes, even if he had the power?

If I were a prince . . . I would rescue them before the third day. The idea leapt into his mind. It would be good to be *doing* something, not just sitting here moping in the dark.

But how can I? I'm not a prince. That was only a story. A lie. I have no power. I can do nothing.

He found his thoughts drifting to Aileen, the widowed mother of Alan of Lynn-by-the-Lake. She had had no power to help her son, nor to stop the townsfolk from hounding him to his death. But in spite of her helplessness, he had sensed in her a kind of strength. *Maybe I can talk to her again. Maybe she can help me. At least talking to a friend would be better than sitting here in misery.* He pushed the box aside and went downstairs. Hedda and Fergus still sat motionless at the table. Hedda looked at him blankly.

"I'm going out," he said gruffly.

"Where? The sun has set and it's almost dark."

"Just out. And the full moon has risen. Soon it will be as bright as day."

Without waiting for a response, he closed the door and strode up the cobbled street along the track that led past the moot ground and across the grazing grounds towards Lynn Lake. By the time he had skirted the bog and was approaching the cottage, he realized that it was indeed dark. The widow lived alone, apart from the rest of the community. Would she even let him in so late, when no sensible person was abroad? Perhaps he had come all this way for nothing.

As he approached the cottage he could see no glimmer of light. The door fit closely, and the single window was shuttered. He knocked and spoke clearly against the wooden planks of the door.

"Aileen, this is Colin, son of Fergus and Hedda. You helped me save my father's ewe. May I come in? I need your help again."

There was no answer, but when at last he stepped back from the door, about to leave, his eyes caught a firefly spark from the chimney, as if she had just stirred up the peat. The door slowly opened.

"Colin? I suppose you may come in." Her tone was grudging.

She was on her knees by the fire as he entered. "Sit," she said, unsmiling, over her shoulder, and went on working the bellows. A small lamp flickered on the table.

"You did not have to return the clothes," she said at last. "They were of no use to me. You must have known that."

"I did. I *was* grateful. I should have liked to have kept them, but Mother made me . . ." His voice trailed off awkwardly into silence.

"You must thank her for the blanket. And for the bread. It was very good." Her voice was cold.

"Mother bakes the best bread in Merton."

She did smile then, a small unwilling smile. "In all of Ariban, I dare say. I used to have a good touch with a loaf myself. But that was before . . . I do not use the village ovens now."

"How can you live without bread?"

"They do not forget to feed me. Bread, fish, milk— all are left regularly at my door. As for the rest, I have my vegetable garden and my herbs. But you haven't come from Merton Town at night to talk about my daily life. What is troubling you, lad?"

"Merton Town held a Moot today," he said abruptly, and she flinched and dropped the bellows with a clatter.

"Who is the victim this time?" she said at last.

"There are two. My little sister Etta and the Stranger, Jennifer. Have you heard of Jennifer?"

"But of course. The storyteller. It was she who returned Alan's clothes and brought the blanket and bread. Well, I am not surprised that she should be persecuted. But your little sister! A child! So what was the verdict of the Moot?"

"For Etta, banishment. For Jennifer . . ." he paused, remembering the death of Alan. "She is to be driven off the cliff," he finished abruptly.

Aileen got to her feet, shaking out her skirt, and began to walk restlessly about the small room. "There was such guilt last time. I did not believe that they would ever . . . not again."

"Guilt?"

"Yes, indeed. Whatever the people of Lynn might tell you, and perhaps even believe themselves, the real reason why I must live alone, why I may not use the village oven or be seen among them, is that they do not want to be continually reminded of the terrible wrong they and the people of Merton Town did to my family. Well, you can see how it would be if I went daily to the well, to the bake oven, to the wash house. They would never be able to forget. So they built this little house by the lake to keep me out of their sight and out of their memory."

"But they still can't forget," Colin said practically. "Since they have to bring you food."

She smiled bitterly. "True, but they do not see my eyes accusing them when they put their offerings secretly on my doorsill." She sighed and sat down again by the fire, holding her thin hands out to its glow. "As for your sister and the storyteller, if you have come to me for advice, I have none to give. It is too late. Jennifer and I had planned that I should hide her here until the merchant ships arrived next full moon and she could smuggle herself aboard. But it is too late now. There is nothing to be done. They have been accused and tried, and the Moot has decided."

"I know." Colin groaned and put his head in his hands. "But there is no one but you I can talk to. You see, it was my fault. I must do *something*, but I don't know what it should be. She had books, you know, as beautiful as—as beautiful as a meadow full of flowers. And her stories . . . Why should stories be so wrong? And dreams? She explained that to me in a kind of story, but it still doesn't make sense."

"Have I not asked myself the same question over and over? Have I not gone through what you are going through? There are times when I hate Ariban and all it stands for. Nights when I cannot sleep and I imagine taking my late husband's boat and stealing away from this wretched island. But it is a hopeless dream. A woman alone! And it takes at least two to handle *Wind Runner*. So I remain in this prison." She laughed bitterly. "And yet I still love Ariban and would sorely miss it," she added. "Which is perhaps the real reason why I am still here."

Colin's attention was caught by her words: stealing away. "Wouldn't they stop you from leaving?"

"They would protest the loss of the boat. She is a good boat, *Wind Runner*. The Elders took her from me when . . . But as for me, they would be glad to see the last of me. Of their guilt."

Colin saw a small glimmer of hope. It had not occurred to him that a person might actually *want* to leave Ariban. "You love Ariban, you say. But you still dream of leaving. Suppose . . . would you consider going into exile with Etta?" he asked abruptly. "I know it is a lot to ask, but I am so afraid for her. She is only a child. What kind of life could she expect, without family or protector? Just thinking of it fills me with horror. She might be better off dead."

Aileen put a hand quickly over his. "Do not speak so."

They sat silently for a while. Colin watched the lamplight flicker across her face. After a while she said thoughtfully, "If we went into exile together, I could say I was her mother. Together we might gain honour, where separately we would be despised. It is a thought. But what of Jennifer? You cannot turn your back on her."

He buried his face in his hands. "I already have.

What can I do now? The decision of the Moot is final. At dawn three days from now—why, it is almost two days already—she will be killed. There is no use talking about it. It is as if it were already done. I burned her books," he added abruptly. "Her beautiful books."

"Why did you do that?"

"To save myself, because I'm a coward. Because it was the Elders' test of my loyalty to Ariban."

Aileen rose and began to pace again.

Once there was a prince, thought Colin again. *Only the prince was not myself. A true prince—what would a true prince do?* The answer came as clearly as if Jennifer were talking to him. *You already know, Colin. A true prince—a real hero—would rescue them from jail and see them safely away from Ariban.*

"But I can't . . ." The words burst out of him.

She stopped her pacing. "What are you thinking? What can you not do?"

He explained his outrageous thought. "It is stupid, I know," he concluded. "This is real life, not a story. The jail is guarded. And even if I could help them escape, they could never leave Ariban. They would soon be captured again and we would all be executed."

She stared at the smouldering peat fire for a while. Then she tightened the shawl about her shoulders and gave a small excited laugh. "There is always *Wind Runner*."

It was his turn to stare. "You said it belonged to the Elders of Lynn."

"I said they *took* it. But it was my husband's—he

built it with his own hands, and I wove the sail and stitched it. It is truly and justly mine for the taking."

It seemed to Colin as if a shutter had swung open in a darkened room to reveal the sun shining outside. "You could sail her?"

"With help. Not by myself. I told you, it takes two. More for a longer journey."

"Jennifer and you. So it *could* be done." Then the imaginary shutter swung shut again, and Colin gave a despairing shrug. "But how could I get them out of jail?"

"Whereabouts is the Merton jail? What is it like?"

"It's just an ordinary one-storey house, in the centre of Merton, close by the well. It has two rooms. The inner one is the cell, and there is a grille between it and the outer room where the jailor sits."

"There is only one jailor?"

"At a time, yes. The townsfolk take it in turns to volunteer. After all, there are seldom any prisoners. I wonder that they bother to have a jail at all."

"Once you make a law saying something is wrong," she replied bitterly, "then the law must be obeyed, and if people break it they must be punished. And if the law is wrong, it is even more necessary that the punishment be seen to work. Therefore Merton Town has a jail."

"Yes." Colin stared at the fire. "Why, I remember being shown the jail and the bars when I was very small. I was told . . . I remember being warned that, if I dreamed made-up stories, I would finish up behind those bars. I had forgotten that."

"And so it goes on," the widow said softly. "For

hundreds of years, perhaps, children have been frightened into forgetting. Till a young woman comes from afar, from a world where dreams are encouraged and storytellers are honoured. Oh, indeed, Colin, my lad, we *must* find a way to rescue both Etta and Jennifer and escape with them from Ariban."

Sudden hope rose in Colin. He spoke rapidly. "I suppose I could wait until the guard fell asleep. But there is a key. I will have to find it. Suppose he were to wake up? Well, perhaps I could hit him over the head. But I don't know if I could."

"You would probably not succeed. In any case violence is wrong and not the answer. I believe I have a better idea." She pointed at the ceiling where hung the bunches of herbs she dried during the summer—aromatic herbs, thyme and mint and rosemary, such as his mother used to flavour her stews of lamb and vegetables. "I think our answer may be there."

"*Cooking* herbs?"

"There are herbs and berries growing on Ariban that have other uses than in the kitchen. This one, for instance, soothes and gives deep sleep to those in pain. The knowledge of these herbs is a skill I learned from my mother. A skill I have kept secret. I did not want to be set apart as a wise woman. From 'wise woman' to 'witch' is but a small step. I searched among my herbs for a cure for Alan's nightmares, but never found it. I could drug him into a dreamless sleep, but not for long—it was too dangerous."

"You're saying you have a potion to make the jailor sleep? Why, that is perfect!"

"It is only an idea, not a plan," the widow cautioned.

"To make it work is another matter entirely. How might you, a member of the suspect family, persuade him to drink it?"

The smile faded from Colin's face. "Yes, I see." Then he found himself asking the new-found story-teller within himself what he should do. And he had the answer. It was really quite simple.

"We have two nights left before . . . before the sentence is carried out. If I were to take some of Hedda's best broth to the jail tomorrow and share it between the jailor and Etta and Jennifer, then he would not be suspicious. And I would promise more the following night."

She nodded. "That is good. But how can you put the herbs only into the bowl from which he will drink? To take proper effect, the herb must infuse in the liquid for at least the time it takes to boil an egg."

Colin thought again. It was strange. First it seemed impossible. Then it slowly became possible. With each "possible" gained, the working out of the next step became easier. "If I had enough herbs to drug all of the broth on the second evening, and if I were to secretly warn Etta and Jennifer not to drink theirs, he would not be suspicious."

"I believe you have hit on the solution." She walked excitedly up and down the small room. "Then you will go back later, once he is deeply asleep, take the key, and release Etta and Jennifer."

"Must they come to Lynn? It is a long way, and they might be discovered."

She shook her head. "No, you're right. That will not work. I have it! As soon as it is dark on the second night, I will go down secretly to the dock where *Wind Runner* is moored. I will take her out and sail her down the coast to Merton Harbour and wait for you there. I will bring provisions and water, clothing and blankets for all four of us."

"*Four*?"

She looked at him in surprise. "Of course. For myself, for you, and for the two girls."

"But . . ." He stared at her blankly. He had not thought past the moment of rescuing Etta and Jennifer. He never imagined *himself* sailing into the unknown aboard a little fishing boat. His future had already been decided. He had been forgiven by the Elders. He was going to build a cottage with his father's help. He was going to marry Gwynne at the Midsummer Festival. He would have his share of his father's flock, and Gwynne would bring her supply of blankets and pots, pans and dishes, as well as a milch goat. And life would go on. They would have children who would grow up on Ariban . . .

"I-I thought it would be only you and the two girls," he stammered. "I would just help you get away."

"It will be far too dangerous for you to stay. Surely you understand that, Colin. You would be suspected at once."

"They could never prove anything. The jailor fell asleep, and they escaped with you. That would be all."

She didn't answer at once, but went to the small chest from which she had taken Alan's clothes. Now she took out a scroll of paper and laid it on the table, flattening it with the weight of dishes on its corners.

"This is Ariban." She pointed, and he leaned over her shoulder to look. It was an old map, judging by the yellowed paper and the faded ink, but it had notes and additions in inks of different shades, as if it had been used and changed over many generations.

"My husband bought this from a trader before we were married. Look, here is Ariban. And here," her finger travelled across the paper, "is the nearest land."

"It doesn't look far."

"The map is small. The distance is great. See, the fishing grounds are over here, barely a tenth of the distance to this other land. It will take at least three days to reach it, perhaps much more if the wind is powerful and contrary. At all times one person must be awake. It is not just for your safety that you must come with us. I need your strong arms and shoulders, Colin, my lad."

Her words were clear. What he must do was clear. If he were to save his sister and Jennifer, there was no other choice. *There was once a prince who left his home to go out into the world . . .*

To leave his mother and father? He remembered the comfort of his mother's lap when he was small and sick with fever. His father's quiet encouragement and steadying hand when he first learned to carve a spoon. The pride in their eyes the first time he brought salvage back from Half-Moon Cove, a timber almost too heavy for him to drag. How could he leave them and the accustomed, ordinary life he had shared with them?

But Etta must go. And Jennifer. Surely he must

have the courage to leave as well. A new thought crept into his mind, a thought that dazzled like the rising sun. *If I go, I will be with Jennifer. And maybe, perhaps, she will forgive me.*

"Give me the herb," he said harshly and stood up, holding out his hand, before he could change his mind.

"Now listen carefully," Aileen told him as she wrapped the dried leaves in a clean cloth and tied it firmly. "I will take *Wind Runner* from her moorings as soon as it is dark enough to be safe. I should be in Merton Harbour soon after moonrise. The tide will have turned by then—well, that cannot be helped— but you *must* be ready and waiting for me so we can be away out of the harbour before the boil."

Colin stared. "What is the 'boil'?"

Aileen stared in turn and then laughed. "I had forgotten that you are the son of a shepherd and not of a fisherman. Listen well, Colin. You know that Merton Harbour is a wide pool with a narrow opening. When the tide floods in, especially when the moon is full—and it will be but two nights after the full of the moon—the sea piles up outside the harbour mouth, unable to push in. It is like trying to pour water into a narrow-necked jug. As it gets closer to high tide the 'boil' becomes more fierce, and it is difficult, if not impossible, to leave the harbour until the tide slackens again. And by then it will be dawn and we will be discovered. Do you understand?"

Colin nodded. "I must get out of the house and free Etta and Jennifer as soon after moonrise as I can. I will do so, Aileen." He tucked the bundle of herbs safely into his jerkin.

"In two nights, then. At Merton Harbour."

"We will be there." He turned at the door and took her hands in his. "Thank you."

She gave a wry smile. "You may thank me when our adventure is done and we are safely come to landfall."

CHAPTER TEN

Two nights later, crouching close to the unshut-
tered southern window of his sister's room,
Colin waited for the moon to rise above the surface
of the dark sea beyond the harbour. It seemed that
he had been waiting forever. No lights showed in
any of the windows of the cottages that lined the
cobbled street leading to the harbour. The only
sound was the continuing murmur of his parents'
voices in their bed alcove in the room below.
Hedda's stony silence had broken at last, and all day
she had lamented. In vain Fergus tried to comfort
her. Now, her lament continued into the night.
Would they *never* go to sleep?

A sliver of silver light ran across the dark water.
He blinked and stared. There it was at last, the rising
moon, lopsided after its fullness of two nights ago.

Was the jailor already sound asleep? Suppose he

wakened from his drugged sleep when Colin searched for the key? Aileen had said, *If he drinks a whole bowl of your mother's broth, he will sleep like a babe till morning. And dream strange dreams that he will forever deny*, she had added with a dry laugh.

It had all gone as he and Aileen had planned. Hedda had willingly aroused herself long enough to cook a big pot of stew and let Colin carry it down to the jail. The jailor's eyes had brightened. "She's a famous cook, is your mother. Can make sheep taste like lamb." He had sat eagerly at the table, elbows out, spooning up the stew.

Colin had managed an easy laugh and said, "But indeed this *is* spring lamb." As he spoke he had backed up towards the bars of the grille that separated the prison cell from the front room. He held his hands behind his back, and in his fingers was a piece of paper. He held it there, his heart jumping, until at last it was twitched from his grasp. With an inward sigh of relief he had left. "I'll be back tomorrow with another potful," he had promised the jailor.

The next day, though, the potful of good broth also contained the sleep herb. He knew Etta and Jennifer would only pretend to eat it, for on the piece of paper—a sheet torn from the back of Hedda's recipe book—he had written in slow crooked capitals: EAT TODAY. TOMORROW DO NOT EAT.

Jennifer would understand. She would have destroyed the paper, and this evening they would have only pretended to eat, spilling their portions into the waste bucket at the back of the cell. Then they would have watched the jailor get more and more sleepy until at last his head fell to the table. That is how it should have gone. If all was well.

Now the moon had risen, and he should be on his way to rescue them.

He glanced anxiously at the horizon. How fast the moon was moving up the sky! Dragged by it, as if in an invisible net, the tide would soon come flooding in. Downstairs he could hear the murmur of voices, broken by his mother's sobs.

Dare I go down and tell them my plan? But then he thought, *Even if they approve, it will be difficult for them to hide the fact that they knew. Then they will be punished for not stopping me. So I must leave secretly, without saying good-bye.*

He had never had to say good-bye. The only good-byes on Ariban were spoken at a person's deathbed. *And I won't even be here with them for that.* His eyes flooded with tears and a sob choked his throat. He took a deep breath and wiped his eyes with his sleeve. "Never" was a harsh word, but one he must learn to live with. *Once there was a prince . . .*

He tried to console himself with the thought that, when morning came, his mother would know that they had escaped, and she would no longer have to mourn. *Except that she will have no children to mother. And Father will have no one to inherit his sheep. And who will look after the two of them in their old age?*

It was a bitter choice to make, but Colin knew it was the right one. "He does not know his path yet," Jennifer had once said, and he had puzzled as to what she meant. Now at last it was clear—as clear as the silver moon-path across the sea. And it was as if a heavy burden had slipped from his shoulders.

He watched the moon creep up the sky. Still his parents talked on. Indeed it seemed likely that they would spend the whole night by the smouldering fire, grieving for their lost daughter.

"Well, I must go, whether they sleep or not," he whispered to himself.

He leaned out of the window. It was a long drop to the ground below. When Etta and Jennifer had escaped from the house, they had used the ladder, but it was now in its usual place behind the house, propped against the thatch. What was he to do?

Then he remembered: since the street sloped steeply upwards towards the grazing grounds, the drop from the north window would be considerably less than from the south.

He tiptoed quietly from Etta's room into his own and pulled open the shutter. The ground was still a long way down, but it was the only possible way out. He tossed his small bundle to the ground outside and, with considerable difficulty, wriggled backwards through the window until he was balanced across the sill, his legs dangling. Slowly he lowered himself, sweating with the effort, until he was dangling at full length, hanging by his fingertips from the sill.

His wet fingers slipped and he dropped unexpectedly, landing unevenly on a tussock of grass, one ankle doubled under him. He grabbed his bundle and scrambled to his feet, then bit back a scream as a stabbing pain ran up his left ankle into his shin.

He bit his lip, pushed back the pain, and began to limp down the street, step by agonizing step.

Hurry, hurry, the moon warned him. Sweat streamed down his face, and he wiped it with his forearm as he tried to walk faster. There was a darkening behind his eyes that warned him of the possibility of fainting. That had happened to him once before, when he had slipped from the roof while helping his father repair the thatch. It had been the left ankle then too, he remembered, and he had had to sit with it bandaged for nigh on six days before it was strong enough to walk on.

Once in the boat, I won't have to use it, he told himself, and struggled on, his bundle thumping uncomfortably against his thigh as he limped.

Now he could see the stone wall around the well. The jail was close by on the left. Very quietly he lifted the latch and pushed open the door. A candle guttered on the table, the wax dribbling down its side. The jailor was sitting with his back to the door, his head on the table, his arms sprawled across it. Colin could hear his faint snore.

Etta gave a squeak, instantly stifled, and he guessed that Jennifer had put a hand over her mouth. Cautiously he approached the sleeping man. Where were the keys? Not in sight on the table. He picked up the dying candle and held it aloft, but he could see little in its glow-worm light. When he had brought the stew, why had he not taken note of where the jailor kept the key? *Stupid!*

A faint whisper came to him out of the shadows. "On the wall. To your left."

And there it was, hanging in plain sight by a leather loop on a peg driven into the stone wall. Quickly he lifted it down and, with hands suddenly clumsy and shaking, inserted it into the padlock that held the grille shut.

An instant later it was open, and they were out. Etta hugged his waist.

"We must hurry," he whispered. "The tide is against us."

Jennifer understood at once, grasped Etta's hand, and pulled her through the door into the street.

Colin extinguished the dying candle between thumb and forefinger and followed them, closing the door carefully behind him. Already the two girls were running lightly down the cobbled street towards the harbour. He limped after them.

Jennifer looked over her shoulder, saw him limping slowly along, and stopped. He waved them frantically forward. She hesitated, then turned and ran silently on, Etta's hand in hers.

The pain was now almost unbearable. Colin leaned against a fisherman's door and took the weight off his ankle for an instant. The respite was wonderful but, when he put his weight on it once more, it hurt even worse than before.

Perhaps it's broken, he thought. *And with no doctoring, I'll be crippled for the rest of my life. I'll be a crippled shepherd—who ever heard of that?* Then he remembered that once he left Ariban, he would no longer even be a shepherd; he had no craft at all.

He tried hopping, but slipped on a rounded cobble

and crashed to the ground, his shoulder hitting some-one's front door with a mighty *thump*. Sobbing and panting, he struggled to his knees. Had anyone heard him? *Perhaps I can crawl*, he thought desperately, and began to scurry spider-like on hands and knees towards the harbour.

High in the eastern sky the moon slipped from behind a cloud, mocking his painful progress, cobble by cobble. Now he could smell the seaweed, the tarri-ness of the fishing nets. Surely he must be nearly there? The hard cobbles ground against his knees, but he crawled on, past house after house.

Suddenly an arm was around his waist, pulling him upright. For a frightening heartbeat he thought he had been caught, but it was only Jennifer. She pulled his arm across her shoulder with a firm grasp on his wrist, and with her other arm around his waist she set out briskly—him hopping beside her—down to the harbour front.

There was the boat, its creamy sail gleaming in the moonlight, bobbing on the tide, seeming impatient to be gone. Etta and Aileen were already aboard, Etta holding the mooring rope, ready to cast it off from the bollard around which it was looped. Aileen stood, oar in hand, anxiously waiting.

"*Hurry!*" The whisper came urgently over the still air. *Still air*. Colin suddenly realized that they could not expect the wind to help them out of the harbour. The sail hung as slackly as a wet wash on the line. They would have to row against the incoming tide.

Jennifer helped Colin aboard, and Etta let go the loose end and coiled the line neatly into the prow of the boat. Aileen pushed *Wind Runner* away from the stone wall and thrust an oar into Colin's hands. "Sit and row—for our lives, boy. Jennifer, take this oar so I can steer. I hope you *can* row, Storyteller."

"Oh, yes. But as for Colin, I don't think he's ever seen the inside of a boat before tonight, have you, Colin? Let the oar lie in the rowlock, like this." She pointed to the metal half hoop cradling her oar. "Now lean forward so the oar goes back above the water. Dig in, but not too deeply, and lean back so the oar moves forward through the water and out at the end of its stroke. Together now, *pull!*"

Facing the stern of the boat, he and Jennifer looked towards the shore. "A light!" he gasped. "So I did wake someone when I fell."

"Keep rowing," Jennifer spoke between clenched teeth. "Harder!"

"The tide's against us," Aileen said. "We've only a short while before the boil forms. Row for your lives, children!"

I still don't really understand what that means, thought Colin. *But I haven't breath enough to ask.*

With one hand on the tiller, the widow leaned forward, pulling first one rope and then another, trying to coax the sail to catch even the smallest puff of wind. The sail shook briefly and then went slack again.

A shout came from ashore, carried clearly across the mirror-still water. "They've discovered us!" Colin panted. Behind him he heard Etta whimper with fear.

"Take heart! They may have *discovered* us, but

they haven't *caught* us yet," Jennifer replied. "Pull on that oar, Colin. Put your heart into it!"

"I am." Colin leaned forward and pulled, and the oar suddenly skimmed the surface in a flurry of spray. He fell back, nearly losing the oar. "Sorry. Sorry."

"Don't worry. Every beginning oarsman does that at least once. Where I come from, it is called 'catching foam'. Breathe slowly, Colin, with your stroke. The skill will come."

"I hope it comes in time," he gasped back. His hands were slippery with sweat, weakening his grip on the oar.

"Can they see us from shore?" the widow asked quietly.

"I expect so," Jennifer replied. "The moon is shining brightly on the sail."

"I was afraid of that. But I did not lower it—I always had the hope that there'd be a breath of wind to catch it."

Colin could feel himself flagging. No matter how hard he tugged on the oar, the boat seemed hardly to move through the water. Then he realized it was not that his muscles were failing, but that the tidal water was beginning to pour into the harbour. Slowly, along the whole coast of Ariban, the water was rising, drawn up by the power of the moon, flooding in towards the shore.

Here, at the entrance to Merton Harbour, where the natural incurving of the shore had been further narrowed by stone walls to north and south, the water was piling up and beginning to spew into the harbour in an angry tumble of waves and eddies.

This must be the "boil" that had worried Aileen. This was what she had warned him about. His lateness in leaving home and his carelessness in twisting his ankle had delayed them so that they had landed in the most dangerous place and time of all. He risked a glance over his left shoulder. The sea wall was close by. Beyond it was the open sea. Between harbour and freedom was a mass of spray and breaking waves: a white barrier. He could hear the voice of the waves now, the angry cry of the sea in all its power, and he was deeply afraid.

I'm no fisherman, he wanted to yell. *I'm a shepherd and I belong on dry land, not out here on these treacherous waves.*

He found himself remembering that last storm, when he had rescued Irving as his sinking boat wallowed in the waves. He remembered, too, how the whole town had watched helplessly while Duff drowned. Duff and his son.

Lean forward, he muttered to himself. *Dig in. Lean back and pull. Lean forward, dig in . . .*

Above the noise of the waves he could hear footsteps pounding along the breakwater to his left. Out of the corner of his eye he could see in the fitful moonlight the shadowy forms of running men.

Why are they running instead of manning their boats? he wondered. *They'll never stop us like that.* Then he realized, with a sudden lift of his spirit, that though the flowing tide might be their enemy, it was also preventing the men of Merton Town from launching their boats and pursuing them.

Now they were almost at the harbour mouth.

Waves dashed against the sides of their boat and broke over them in showers of spray. In the stern, the widow had her feet braced against a rib as she leaned on the tiller and tugged at the sail rope. A gust shivered the sail. A wave broke over the bow.

"Hold tight and stay low, little Etta," Aileen shouted over the tumult of the waves. Colin hoped that she had heard and was obeying, but he dared not turn his head to look.

The men were at the end of the southern breakwater now. As the moon slipped from behind a cloud, Colin could see them shaking their fists. A stone thudded against the side of the boat, and another one bounced inside. He felt a sharp blow on his shoulder and tightened his grip on his oar. If a lucky throw should knock Aileen unconscious, they would be lost. Or if one should make a hole in the bottom of the boat!

He looked down fearfully at the planks beneath his legs. Water washed to and fro, and his heart leapt in sudden panic. But as another wave broke over the side, he realized that that's all it was. They weren't sinking. They were shipping water, but they weren't going to sink.

Suddenly, as they struggled to cross the barrier of waves and incoming tide in the white chop at the harbour entrance, a strong gust of wind came out of the west and caught the sail. It filled out into a creamy arc above their heads, and *Wind Runner* began to live up to its name. As they raced away from the shore, the oar was nearly torn from Colin's grasp. He pulled it free of the water and out of the rowlock, sliding it to safety along the bottom boards.

"Well done!" Aileen called out. "You can rest now. The wind will do the work and take us wherever we want to go."

"Where is that?" Colin shouted back. "Has it got a name, this land we're sailing to?"

"I expect it has. We will find out what *they* call it when we arrive. In the meantime, my name for it is Freedom."

"And mine is Once-upon-a-Future," added Jennifer. "What is your name for the new land, Etta?"

"Oh, I think I will call it Storyland. What about you, Colin?"

But he only shook his head. How could he tell them that the only name he had for the new world to which they were heading was Not-Ariban? He had done what had to be done. He had indeed saved Etta and Jennifer, and perhaps, in persuading Aileen to take them in *Wind Runner*, had also rescued her from the half death of her widow's exile on the muddy shores of Lynn Lake. He was a hero, after all. But the taste of it was very bitter in his mouth.

"Colin?" Etta persisted.

"Hush, Etta." Jennifer spoke so gently that he wondered if she guessed what he was feeling. "Colin, now that there is time, I must bandage your ankle."

"You will find linen strips in the medicine box amidships," Aileen said. "Once his ankle is bound up, you had best bail out the water we shipped during that rough passage."

So Colin's ankle was bandaged—he found Jennifer's hands comfortingly gentle and firm, though he could not talk to her and found it hard to meet her eye. Then together they scooped up water from the bottom boards in bailing pans, throwing it over the side until the inside of the boat was nearly dry.

"There are blankets in that linen bag near the prow," Aileen directed. "Wrap yourselves up and sleep for the rest of the night. I need no help so long as the wind continues to blow from the west."

Without argument they wrapped themselves up and snuggled down as best they might on the bottom boards, and, rocked by the steady motion of the boat, all three slept.

Colin woke with the sun on his face and with a bewildering feeling of displacement. Why was his bed so hard? Why was the room so bright? Hadn't he closed his shutter before sleeping? A twinge of pain in his ankle brought a flood of memory. He sat up abruptly, throwing off his cocoon of blanket.

In the prow Etta still slept, a small figure rolled in her blanket. Beyond her the blue sea reached up to an infinite blue sky. He turned. Jennifer, too, was sleeping, her hands folded under her cheek, her dark hair trailing across her face. In the stern Aileen sat at ease, one hand on the tiller, her eyes on the horizon.

Behind her was nothing but the same platter of blue sea reaching up to the bowl of blue sky. There was no Ariban. There was nothing in any direction but a blue emptiness, with themselves an insignificant dot in the midst of it. There were no clouds. There was nothing to indicate that they were moving, except for the full curve of *Wind Runner*'s square sail. He put his hand over the side and felt the cold water race over his fingers. It was strange. Lonely. Terrifying.

If only I were watching the sheep, mending the thatch, fetching fodder for the goats . . . He shut his eyes, imagining the firm ground beneath his feet.

"Come, Colin. Take the tiller." Aileen roused him from his longing for Ariban. "I will find something to break our fast before I sleep."

He crawled gingerly towards the stern, afraid that at any instant the boat would tip and send him helplessly into the water. His twisted ankle hardly hurt at all now. He sat beside her. "What do I do?"

"Your hand here." She placed it on the tiller, hers over it, and he felt its aliveness, the aliveness of the whole boat. It made him shiver.

"Now watch the sail. See how full it is, with no wrinkles in it. If I move the tiller this way, notice how it begins to fall limp. And if I move it the other way, see how the wrinkles lie?" She moved the tiller slightly so that the sail was once more round and full. "Now keep it so."

She took away her guiding hand, and Colin sat tensely on the edge of the stern thwart, staring at the sail. Little by little he began to relax. He could feel *Wind Runner* respond to the wind, her prow cutting through the gentle waves. She moved like a living thing. Before long he found that he could tell that they were still on course, not by staring at the sail but by the feel of the wind on his cheeks. The sea began to seem less lonesome, less fearful. He looked up again at the creamy sail and felt the warmth of the sun on his face. He found that he was smiling, though he didn't know why.

The others woke, yawning and stretching, as Aileen moved around amidships. She brought out of her storage chest bread and cheese and a flask of water for them to share. *Wind Runner* skimmed on, and the sun slowly swung into the southern sky.

Aileen slept and later woke, and they ate another frugal meal. Jennifer and Etta talked in low tones. Colin sat in peaceful silence, his hand on the tiller, feeling the boat move under him. He was no longer arguing with himself. No longer plotting how best to serve himself. He had moved past all that into a time-less space of blue sea and blue sky—a space without deception, without lies.

At twilight Aileen again took the helm, and the other three fell asleep as if they had spent their whole lives in boats, with bare boards for beds. The next day passed in the same way, but when they woke on the third day, it was to see a line of grey along the eastern horizon.

"Will it storm?" Colin asked. "Is it bad?"

Aileen shaded her eyes and peered anxiously ahead. Then she laughed and there was relief in her laughter. "Not storm clouds, Colin, my lad. Landfall!"

"We really are safe now, aren't we? We can begin a whole new life. Storyland," chimed in Etta. "A home for a storyteller. But Jennifer, what will you do without your books?"

In the silence that followed, Colin felt his cheeks burn. The freedom and happiness he had known during the two previous magic days vanished, and the familiar guilt overwhelmed him once more. The evil he had done could never be undone. The books destroyed. Etta forever banished. His parents left to face their old age, childless. Gwynne . . . *No*, he decided. *Gwynne I do not regret.*

In the midst of his misery, he remembered the small bundle he had dragged painfully through the town and stowed aboard. Now was the time for it. He searched for it and held it out to Jennifer: his guilt offering.

"F-forgive me for betraying you," he stammered. "For destroying your books. I know there is nothing I can ever do to replace them. This is all I have of yours. The story box. It is nothing, I know, but . . ." His voice trailed off into silence.

"Oh, but it is!" Jennifer's face lit up as she took the box from him and held it between her hands. Lovingly she stroked the carved surface.

Colin took the key from around his neck, where he had kept it tucked inside his shirt ever since the box had been returned to him after the Moot.

Now he handed it to her. Solemnly Jennifer unlocked the box and slowly lifted the lid. She looked within. Then, with both hands, she reached down into its emptiness and brought her hands up, cupped together as if they were holding some precious treasure.

She looked into her hands and then up at the blue sky, at the creamy sail swelling in the wind. At the approaching line of dark along the horizon that grew ever more distinct . . .

"Once upon a time," she began, "there was a widow woman sorrowing for her dead son; a girl child who fought with dragons; a young hero puzzling over who he really was; a storyteller escaping from a shipwreck. Together they sailed across the wide ocean towards a new land. A land of stories and dreaming. A land of imagination and beauteous images . . ."

Wind Runner sped over the water. The sun moved slowly into the western sky, and the coast ahead grew ever closer as her story came to an end.

". . . and so they came at last to their beginning."

Jennifer tipped her empty hands back into the story box and closed the lid.

ABOUT THE AUTHOR

© Ian Grant Inc.

Monica Hughes, a writer of international acclaim, was born in England and now lives in Edmonton, Alberta. A writer who constantly challenges both herself and her readers and who writes with equal skill in different genres, she is the author of more than 30 books, including *Invitation to the Game*, *The Seven Magpies*, and, most recently, *The Other Place*. Her numerous literary awards include the Vicky Metcalf Award. In 1982 and 1983, she received the Governor General's Award, then known as the Canada Council Prize for Children's Literature.